VORDAK
THE INCOMPREHENSIBLE

RULE THE SCHOOL

EGMONT
USA
New York

EGMONT

We bring stories to life

First published by Egmont USA, 2011
443 Park Avenue South, Suite 806
New York, NY 10016

Copyright © Scott Seegert, 2011
Illustrations by John Martin
All rights reserved

1 3 5 7 9 8 6 4 2

www.egmontusa.com
www.vordak.com

Library of Congress Cataloging-in-Publication Data is available
LCCN number: 2011021030
ISBN 978-1-60684-014-6
eBook ISBN 978-1-60684-280-5

Printed in the United States of America
Text and page layout by Arlene Schleifer Goldberg

CPSIA tracking label information:
Printed in June 2011 at Berryville Graphics, Berryville, Virginia

DEDICATION

As some of you may recall, I dedicated my first book to myself. It was brought to my attention that this was a sign of inflated self-importance and extreme egomania—which is why I am also dedicating this book to me.

ACKNOWLEDGMENTS

I would be remiss if I failed to mention the efforts of my agent, Dan Lazar, my editor, Regina Griffin, and all the fine professionals at Writers House and Egmont USA. Folks, your efforts were deplorable.

OBSERVATIONAL POETRY

As I peruse the pages
Of my scintillating sequel
I am once again reminded
I'm a writer without equal.

Contents

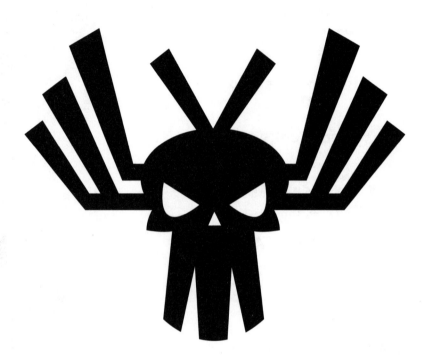

PUT THIS BOOK DOWN
IMMEDIATELY!

I DON'T KNOW WHO YOU THINK YOU ARE
OR WHY YOU CONSIDER YOURSELF WORTHY
OF READING MY WONDROUS WORDS,
BUT I REFUSE TO ALLOW YOUR GRUBBY
LITTLE CHEEZ-DOODLE–STAINED FINGERS
TO TARNISH THE PERFECT PAGES OF THIS . . .

Hold on a minute. I'll be right back.

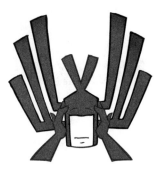

*ALL RIGHT, VORDAK. CALM
DOWN. YOU PROMISED THAT
YOU WOULD TRY TO BE NICE
TO THE READERS THIS TIME
AROUND. THAT YOU WOULD
BE RESPECTFUL OF THEM.
NOW LET'S TRY THIS AGAIN.*

Why, hello there, valued reader! I'm back. And it is
both an honor and a privilege to have a bright young
person such as yourself browsing through my humble
little book. I can't thank you enough for taking time
out of your busy day to . . . . . . *ACK!* Forget it! I would

rather yank my spleen out through my nostrils than continue with this charade!

Look, we both know you don't deserve to thumb through the pages of my treasured tome. Rules are rules, however, and since you purchased the book, I can't stop you from reading it. But don't expect me to "dummy" things down just so you can understand them. I am, after all, an Evil ~~Supergeneous~~ ~~Supergenious~~ *Supergenius*!

Despite your best efforts to annoy me, my mood refuses to be dampened, as I am in the midst of what will surely become the most immeasurably magnificent day of my or any other life! You see, after years of hard work and spoiled plans, I am mere moments away from accomplishing two of my three most cherished Evil Goals:

VORDAK THE INCOMPREHENSIBLE'S

Lip-Lickingly Loathsome List
of Most Cherished Evil Goals

1. Dispose of my arch-nemesis, Commander Virtue, once and for all.

2. Take over and Rule the World!

3. Make all escalators travel only in the downward direction (MUAHAHAHAHA!!!).

I still have no idea how to go about number 3, but the first two are finally within my grasp. And I envy you. Yes, as strange as that may seem, *I*, Vordak the Incomprehensible, actually envy *you*, a random doofus.

Why? Because you are about to witness these astounding events firsthand! I have personally seen myself achieve the unthinkable many times, but you, YOU, will be experiencing it for the very *first* time. You have my permission to pass out from the sheer excitement of it all. Go ahead—I'll wait.

. . . .

Welcome back. Now, I'm sure you're wondering why, with ultimate success so near at hand, I am sitting here in a junior high school auditorium, surrounded by beings much younger than myself.

"Not really. I had no idea you were even _in_ an auditorium."

Of course you didn't! If it was my desire for you to know my whereabouts, you would. But it's not, so you don't.

"Well, you're the one who said I was wondering why you were in the—"

Okay, just stop it! If you insist upon droning on this way, we won't get anywhere. It happens to be Career Day at the school and I'm crammed into this auditorium listening to various parents ramble on about what they do for a living.

That's Commander Virtue on the left. That's right—*THE* Commander Virtue. Right here onstage! Just look at that costumed clump of conceit, smiling away as if he hadn't a care in the world, just waiting for his opportunity to step to the podium and be showered with undeserved applause. Oh, how I despise that clown!

No, not *that* clown. That's Silvia Glupner's father. He wasted fifteen minutes of my valuable time demonstrating how to walk in floppy shoes. I'm talking about Commander Virtue. Although, to tell you the truth, I'm not real pleased with Glupner right now, either.

Virtue doesn't realize it yet, but I have made sure this will be his last public appearance—EVER! What do you think of that?

. . . .

I said WHAT DO YOU THINK OF THAT?!

"Oh, sorry. I finished reading for now and was just bending the corner of the page to mark my place."

WHAT?! How can you possibly put the book down *now*, with such a monumental moment at hand? Perhaps you do not fully understand the importance of what is about to happen. Perhaps you need to know what I went through to get to this point in order to truly appreciate what you are about to witness. Perhaps, since we have a few minutes before Commander Virtue addresses the crowd, I will fill you in on the events of the past eight weeks. Perhaps you will be eternally grateful for my doing so. Perhaps you will remember how to spell *perhaps* correctly since you've seen it so many times in this paragraph. Perhaps you had better move on to the *next* paragraph so we can get started. I don't have all day.

And by the way—if I ever catch you disfiguring my book again by creasing a page corner, I will dispatch my Book Retrieval Bot to your home to reclaim my Wondrous Work. Don't worry—you shall remain unharmed during the process.

Perhaps.

Before I continue, I suppose there could be one or two readers out there who do not know who I am. To those individuals I would simply like to introduce myself as Vordak the Incomprehensible and say . . . *SERIOUSLY*?! How in the name of Zaldok the Inconceivable have you never heard of Vordak the Incomprehensible?! My Supervillainous exploits have been the stuff of legend! Seriously, just how pathetic a person must you be to remain unaware of my treasure trove of tyrannical triumphs? Frankly, you should be ashamed of yourself.

Unfortunately, I don't have the time to properly convey to you the magnificence that is me. Not if I am to do my story justice. So turn the page to find my bio from the Registry of Supervillains to help bring you up to speed.

REGISTRY OF SUPERVILLAINS
(Please print clearly)   #372

Evil Supervillain Name (attach photo)	*Vordak the Incomprehensible*
Real Name	*That IS my real name!*
Location of secret lair	~~24319 Elmh~~ *Hey! How stupid do you think I am?*
Parents	*Walter and Irene the Incomprehensible*
Pets	*Armageddon - my genetically altered dog*
Superpowers	*Incomprehensibility*
Evil Laugh type	*MUAHAHAHAHA!!*
Other attributes	*Incredible intelligence, immeasurable handsomeness, humbleness*

Evil Goals
(check all that apply)

- ☐ Destroy the earth
- ☐ Destroy the universe
- ☒ Rule the World
- ☒ Rid the world of your arch-nemesis
- ☒ Other (list)

  Increase the standard school day to 13 hours

  Make ASPARAGUS the only ice cream flavor available

Arch-nemesis. (attach photo)	*Commander Virtue*
Description	*Stupid, fat, ugly jerk who I hate*
How do you attempt to dispose of him/her?	*Diabolically clever yet extremely slow-acting death traps*
Have you ever succeeded?	*No*
I didn't think so	*What's THAT supposed to mean?!*
It was just a hunch	*A hunch, huh?! Well, at least I'm not some pathetic little registry questionnaire!*

Oh yeah? Well PPHHHFFTTTTT to you, pal. And guess what - I'm not giving you a line to respond on! Nana nana boo boo!

"Wait a minute. I thought you were a RETIRED Supervillain. And now you're back to trying to Rule the World? What's going on?"

Well, that's *your* fault. It's been almost a year since I wedged my Glorious Guide to Supervillainy, *How to Grow Up and Rule the World*, into the eagerly awaiting hands of millions of hopeful young planet conquerors—*and none of you has managed to Rule the World yet*! In fact, I have the feeling some of you *haven't even read it at all*! I mean, what's up with *that*? I don't know exactly what the problem is, but it's certainly nothing on my end. I offered every teeny-tiny bit of information one could possibly require to seize control of the earth . . . and you dropped the ball. Every single one of you.

Would I rather have had one of *you* conquer the planet and make me your second in command so I could then have taken over ~~when~~ if you met your "unexpected" demise? Of course. But that didn't happen. And I grew impatient. So I decided to take matters into my own hands . . .

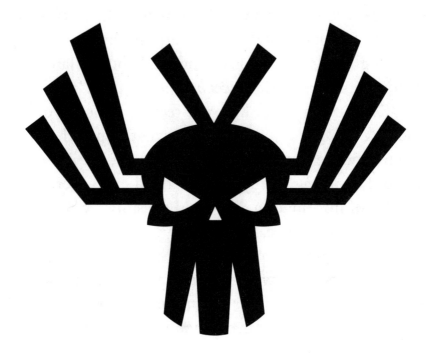

CHAPTER ONE

Eight Weeks Ago

The thought came to me in a single instant of evil inspiration—I WILL CREATE THE MOST POWERFUL FREEZE RAY THE WORLD HAS EVER KNOWN AND USE IT TO TURN ALL THE WATER ON THE ENTIRE PLANET TO ICE! MUAHAHAHAHA!!! Unfortunately, I have no idea how to create a ray to do *that*. Sure, I'm brilliant and all, but, c'mon now. That's asking a lot even from me. So I'll *threaten* to do it. All I really need to do is freeze a smaller body of water, for example Lake Chargoggagoggmanchauggagoggchaubunagungamaugg (it's in Massachusetts—look it up), to scare the planet into surrendering. Ah, the mere thought of conquering the earth had my evil blood boiling once again!

I couldn't wait to get started!

It was pretty obvious that my time away from active Supervillainy had left me a bit out of shape. If I was to regain the energy necessary to implement my freeze-ray plan and RULE THE WORLD, I had two options:

1. Switch to a diet of fruits and vegetables and follow a daily exercise routine that would allow me to gradually get into better condition.

2. Develop some diabolical device that would instantly make me younger.

After a great deal of thought (mainly about how much I despise vegetables and exercise), I chose to go with option 2, which I decided to call my *Yolk-Yellow Youth Machine*! MUAHAHAHAHA!!!

"That's lame."

Yes, I know. Even *with* the evil laugh. Plus, it's not actually yellow. So, I *re*-decided to name it my *Yoo-Hoo, How Do You Do Yickety-Yackety Youth Machine*! MUAHAHAHAHA!!!

"That's even LAMER."

I'd like to see you do better! Those *Y*s are tricky little critters, which is why I finally settled on *Abominable Age-Reduction Ray*. Not my best effort, I admit, but it does get the point across.

**"Well, since you retired from Supervillainy years ago,
where did you get the money for your freeze ray
and your 'youth' machine?"**

My, you are a nosey little numbskull, aren't you?
Why, from the sales of my first book, of course. It turns
out that all the effort I put into the creation of that
Maliciously Magnificent Manual (see—I'm much better
with *M*s) paid off after all. Even though the book did
not produce a planetary dictator as I had hoped, I did
receive nearly enough cash to fund my own return to
Supervillainy. (Going door-to-door collecting returnable
bottles and cans provided the rest.) Of course, I had to
spend half of it to expand my lair.

Yes, that's right. I have been living in my parents'
house. What's it to you? It's been tough out there
for former Supervillains. Besides, I shipped Mom
and Dad out to a retirement community months
ago, so I have the place all to myself. And, with my
new expansion, I once again have a lair worthy of my
overwhelmingly overwhelming overwhelmingness.
MUAHAHAHAHA!!! Now, if you will stop with the
inane interruptions, I can get back to my story.

Before

After

I spent the next few days diligently designing my decidedly diabolical devices. I wasn't too concerned about the Fantastically Frigid Freeze Ray since I had created plenty of less powerful freeze rays in the past. The Abominable Age-Reduction Ray was going to be a first, however. Oh, I had designed and unleashed upon the hapless heaps of humanity all manner of menacing machines—shrink rays, growth rays, mind-control rays, even my Wondrously Wicked Worm Ray (more on that later)—but never an Age-Reduction Ray. This was going to take some real evil effort on my part.

To make matters worse, you can't build one without a balsoid coil, which is extremely difficult to find. They were last used commercially on 1953 Clean-O-Matic dishwashers. After days of searching, one of my henchmen finally located a coil on a shelf behind the furnace in the basement of an old, abandoned Clean-O-Matic warehouse in Tutwiler, Mississippi. As a reward for his faithful service, I awarded him the highest honor possible for a lackey of Vordak the Incomprehensible.

He was the envy of the henchman community.

With the balsoid coil in place, I began by testing the ray on a rock. Looking back, I'm not sure why.

Before

After

Next was a chicken. This time the results were excellent.

Before

After

Feeling rather confident, I proceeded to a human subject.

Before

After

Again, excellent results, although it was clear I needed to adjust the settings just a tad. Normally, I would have performed one final test on a more intelligent life form, like a cucumber, but I was growing impatient. I had seen enough to declare my Abominable Age-Reduction Ray a complete success and decided to use it on *myself* right then and there.

> *"Uh, I have a feeling that wasn't a good idea."*

OF COURSE it was a good idea! When have I ever had one that wasn't?

> *"What about the time you turned yourself into an ostrich so you could escape the island prison of Platzvaria?"*

Well, how was I supposed to know that ostriches can't fly? Or swim very well? Or that Platzvarians consider ostrich burgers to be a delicacy? Anyway, I used the ray on myself.

Okay, sure, I overshot my age target. No big deal. All I had to do was reverse the setting and try again. Why the smug look on your face?

"Because I read ahead to the next paragraph (snicker)."

That's cheating! Normally I would applaud such behavior, but not when it's done against *me*! If I catch you doing that again, you'll be receiving a visit from the Book Retrieval Bot. All right—you looked ahead. So you already know that during the process of shrinking me down, my Age-Reduction Ray blew its balsoid coil.

Meaning I was stuck like this until I could find another one.

WIPE THAT SMIRK OFF YOUR FACE!

CHAPTER TWO

Seven Weeks Ago

This really wasn't as bad as I thought it would be. In fact, it was kind of fun! Things didn't start out so well—it's difficult to get anything accomplished when you can't see out of your helmet and your utility belt is wrapped around your knees—but, luckily, Mom had saved my old costume in a box in the attic.

No, I wasn't going to strike fear in the hearts of humanity looking like this. I couldn't even reach the gas pedal in my Spiderbot, for crying out loud. But there were so many other things I *could* do. Like watch cartoons. And play video games. And eat hot dogs dipped in chocolate without getting sick. And get into movie theaters for half price.

Using my Befuddling Balsoid Coil Detector, I had located a replacement balsoid coil. At one point I lost the detector itself but found it using my Befuddling *Befuddling Balsoid Coil Detector* Detector. As luck would have it, the only coil within a two-thousand-mile radius happened to be located somewhere within the woebegone walls of Farding Junior High School, a scant mile and a half from my lair! I would need to find a way to retrieve that coil, but that could wait. I had more playing to do.

I never even knew I liked video games. Their carnage and destruction always seemed boring compared to the real thing. Now I couldn't put that little controller down. I had just settled in to a rousing round of my favorite game when the doorbell rang.

WHO DARES INTERRUPT MY GAME MID-KICK?!

HELLO THERE, YOUNG MAN. ARE YOUR PARENTS HOME?

MOST LIKELY.

MAY I SPEAK WITH THEM?

I DON'T SEE WHY NOT.

I shut the door. I had no idea who that troglodyte was, but if he wanted my parents, he would have to head over to their retirement community and talk to them. The doorbell rang again.

I REALLY NEED TO SPEAK WITH YOUR PARENTS. COULD YOU ASK THEM TO COME TO THE DOOR?

WHAT, YOU MEAN THIS DOOR? THAT COULD TAKE A WHILE.

WHY, ARE THEY IN THE MIDDLE OF SOMETHING?

NOW, HOW WOULD I KNOW THAT? YOU HAD BEST LEAVE. MY PATIENCE IS WEARING THIN.

I shut the door again, this time with more force. The nerve of some people—thinking they can just saunter up to my lair and interrupt my very important video game with nonsensical chitchat. I made a mental note to install a trapdoor in the porch at my first opportunity. The doorbell rang yet again.

LOOK HERE, YOUNG MAN. MY NAME IS TRUANCY OFFICER MORTNER. ONE OF YOUR NEIGHBORS REPORTED SEEING A SCHOOL-AGED CHILD RUNNING AROUND THE PREMISES WHEN HE SHOULD HAVE BEEN IN CLASS, AND IT APPEARS SHE WAS RIGHT. I NEED TO TALK TO YOUR PARENTS NOW.

One of my neighbors? That old busybody Mrs. Brundlefly, no doubt! The last thing I needed right then was to draw attention to myself, so I calmly explained the situation.

AH, MORTNER, THERE SEEMS TO BE SOME SORT OF MISUNDERSTANDING. YOU SEE, I AM ACTUALLY AN ADULT. I HAVE TAKEN ON THIS APPEARANCE TEMPORARILY DUE TO A MALFUNCTION OF MY ABOMINABLE AGE-REDUCTION RAY. I'M SURE YOU UNDERSTAND.

OH, SURE. THOSE AGE-REDUCTION RAYS CAN BE TRICKY. WHY, JUST YESTERDAY I WAS . . . GET YOUR PARENTS OUT HERE RIGHT THIS MINUTE!

Mortner was mocking me! That bald-headed bumpkin was actually mocking ME, Vordak the Incomprehensible! I had lost all patience with the man. It was time to put my near limitless brain power to work and devise, as only I can, an incredibly clever, breathtakingly brilliant, exceedingly sensational scheme to rid myself of this chubby-chinned chatterbox once and for all.

THERE'S A SPIDER ON YOUR SHOE.

As he was sprinting back down the driveway, Mortner tossed the enrollment forms over his shoulder and shouted that they needed to be filled out and that, if I wasn't in class by the beginning of the next week, we would be hauled into court. There was no way I was getting in front of a judge. What if he figured out who I really was? And all the diabolical deeds I had done? I'm fairly certain there are stiff penalties for hollowing out Mount Rushmore and using it as an Evil Lair. Or filling the Grand Canyon with strawberry Jell-O.

I needed to keep a low profile and, no matter how much fun I was having, I also needed to return to my normal nasty self. So, now I had *two* problems to deal with—at the same time! In situations like this, I find that if I write the problems down and stare at them for hours on end, the solution usually becomes clear:

```
Problem 1.   Must figure out a way to get
             inside Farding Junior High
             School in order to get my
             hands on the balsoid coil.

Problem 2.   Must figure out what to do
             with this enrollment form
             for Farding Junior High
             School.
```

Nope. Nothing was coming to me at the moment.

**"Why didn't you just fill out the enrollment form
and become a student?"**

And why don't you just quit stealing my brilliant
ideas?! I said nothing was coming to me *at the
moment*. Enrolling in the school is *exactly* what I did.
Eventually. I figured I would get in, locate the balsoid
coil, and get out. It shouldn't take more than a day
or two. What the heck, I might even have a little fun
while I was there. After all, I thought, it was junior
high—how hard could it be?

CHAPTER THREE

Six Weeks Ago

EXTREMELY HARD!

Junior high proved to be much more of a pain than I remembered. In fact, just getting there was a challenge. I couldn't very well drive myself in my present condition. Law enforcement does not look favorably upon twelve-year-olds driving motor vehicles on public roads. I found that out the hard way when I really *was* twelve. I could have had one of my henchmen drive me, but I don't trust them at the controls of my toaster, much less one of my villainous vehicles. And walking a mile and a half was certainly out of the question, as I have already pointed out my distaste for exercise. That left . . . the bus.

Monday arrived and I loaded up my backpack with everything I would require for my first day of school, including my portable Befuddling Balsoid Coil Detector. When the bus arrived, I decided to sit up front so I could get off quickly. The less time spent in that yucky yellow yo . . . in that yippety yellow ya . . . (ACK! Again with the *Y*s—first it was the youth machine and now this. Speaking with the vibrant vocabulary of villainy can be a real pain at times. Must . . . concentrate. . . .) The less time spent in that cramped, canary-colored carrier (YES!) the better. The other passengers all tried their best to cram into the rear of the bus, where all the "cool" kids sit. All, that is, save one—Myron H.—whose name I figured out without even using my powers of incomprehensibility.

Now, I am used to having ordinary humans stare at me in awe. I often demand it, in fact. But Myron H. was creeping me out. And he never uttered a word the entire trip. Just sat there . . . motionless . . . staring. I thought he might have been a robot.

A lousy morning got worse once I arrived at my dreadful destination.

It turns out the school had a security checkpoint just inside the entrance. This was unfortunate.

They even took my portable Befuddling Balsoid Coil Detector! If I was to find that prized appliance part now, I was going to have to do it the old-fashioned way—by capturing the principal and dangling him over a pit of particularly peeved pythons until he reveals its location. MUAHAHAHAHA!!! Unfortunately, after asking around a bit, I was appalled to discover that this sorry excuse for a school doesn't even *have* a python, peeved or otherwise. So I was now forced to resort to the *old*-old-fashioned way, which mainly involves sneaking around when no one is looking. This was going to take longer than I thought.

Before I could officially begin my first day of school, I had to meet with the principal to go over all my paperwork. Imagine—Vordak the Incomprehensible having to prove himself worthy of attending junior high to some slack-jawed simpleton.

"Um, I hope you didn't call him that to his face."

Oh, I wanted to, but I needed to play it cool. Yes, he was clearly my inferior and the very thought of carrying on a conversation with him made my brain throb in agony, but sometimes you do what you must. I took a seat across from his desk and concentrated on staying polite and under control for as long as was necessary. I am Vordak the Incomprehensible! Nothing is beyond my capability!

HELLO, YOUNG MAN. MY NAME IS MR. COMBOVER. AND YOU MUST BE VODRAK.

 IT'S VORDAK, YOU SLACK-JAWED SIMPLETON!

"Ha! I knew it!"

Well, aren't you a little smarty-pants. Anyway, as punishment, Combover had me spend the next thirty minutes closely examining the wallpaper seam in the corner of his office. That's right, no giant circular saws or vats of acid or tanks filled with scorpions. I decided Combover would make a terrible Supervillain. When the thirty minutes were up, I returned to my seat across from his desk.

NOW, LET'S TRY THIS AGAIN, SHALL WE? AS I SAID, MY NAME IS MR. COMBOVER, AND I'M THE PRINCIPAL HERE AT FARDING JUNIOR HIGH.

 WHAT IN GRIMNOR'S NAME IS A FARDING?

IT'S NOT A WHAT. IT'S A WHO. FREDERICK FARDING WAS THIS COUNTRY'S TOP TRAINER OF SOLDIERS DURING WORLD WAR II. LEGEND HAS IT THE ENEMY WOULD TURN AND RUN IF THEY SO MUCH AS SNIFFED A FARDING SOLDIER.

 AS WOULD I.

YOUR PAPERWORK SEEMS TO BE IN ORDER, ALTHOUGH I DO HAVE A FEW QUESTIONS CONCERNING THE "PREVIOUS INJURIES" YOU LISTED ON THE HEALTH HISTORY FORM. HOW EXACTLY DOES ONE SUSTAIN A "TORN RIGHT NOSTRIL"?

ACK! I should have known he would ask about this. I've suffered a multitude of miserable mishaps over the years while battling Commander Virtue. In order to avoid raising suspicion, I would have to use my inconceivable intellect to carefully craft a set of diabolically detailed lies to explain how I received those injuries.

I TRIPPED OVER A ROCK.

AND THE FLATTENED INTESTINES?

TRIPPED OVER A ROCK.

I SEE. . . . SCALDED BUTTOCKS? LET ME GUESS—YOU TRIPPED OVER A ROCK.

AN EXTREMELY HOT ROCK.

YOU SEEM TO HAVE A HUGE PROBLEM KEEPING YOUR BALANCE.

 WELL, MY HELMET IS FAIRLY HEAVY.

AND THAT BRINGS ME TO MY NEXT POINT. HELMETS WITH METAL ANTLERS . . .

 BLADES!

VERY WELL, HELMETS WITH METAL "BLADES" ARE TOO DANGEROUS TO WEAR TO SCHOOL. AND CAPES ARE A CHOKING HAZARD. I'M AFRAID YOU WON'T BE ABLE TO WEAR YOUR COSTUME TO SCHOOL AGAIN AFTER TODAY.

 WHAT?! RARELY HAVE I EVER CHOKED ANYONE WITH MY CAPE! AND WITHOUT MY HELMET OF DISCONCERTMENT, EVERYONE WILL BE ABLE TO SEE MY FACE! I PREFER TO MAINTAIN A CERTAIN LEVEL OF SECRECY.

WELL, RULES ARE RULES, I'M AFRAID. THE ONLY WAY YOU COULD CONTINUE TO WEAR YOUR COSTUME IS IF YOU HAD A DOCTOR'S PERMISSION DUE TO A MEDICAL CONDITION. ANYWAY, DON'T WORRY ABOUT IT. ONCE YOU GET USED TO IT, I THINK YOU'LL FIND FARDING TO BE A WONDERFUL EXPERIENCE.

 **I ALREADY DO.**

I spent the rest of that first day getting comfortable with the layout of the school. There was no sign of the balsoid coil—so much for it just lying about in the open. I would begin my search in earnest the next day.

. . . .

Since it appeared I would be spending more time than I'd originally planned at the school, I decided to hire an Evil Scientist to get started on the Fantastically Frigid Freeze Ray. Even though my expanded lair is in pretty good shape, I have not yet had the time to rebuild my evil organization. I did pick up a couple of henchmen who were looking for a new Evil Mastermind after their former leader, The Black Corpuscle, was captured by Commander Virtue, but that's it as of now. So I placed an ad in *The Criminal Chronicle*:

HELP WANTED

Super-intellectual to serve as Evil Genius for world-renowned Supervillain. Must have his own lab coat and calculator and an enormous head that makes it look like he's always about to tip over. Experience with freeze rays a plus. Contact V THE I, whereabouts unknown.

Unfortunately, only one person answered the ad, a guy named Professor Cranium. The fact that he was able to locate my secret lair spoke well for his intelligence. The fact that his pants were on backwards did not. I couldn't afford to be choosy, however, so I brought him on board.

The good news is Myron H. didn't sit next to me on the bus Tuesday morning. The bad news is Fara Farkesh, who is apparently undergoing some sort of major orthodontic procedure, did.

MIND IF WE SHARE A SHEAT? SHAY, YOU MUSHT BE THAT NEW SHTUDENT. I'M FARA FARKESH. SHO, HOW DO YOU LIKE SHCHOOL SHO FAR? SHOME SHTUDENTSH SHAY I TALK TOO MUCH, BUT I SURE DON'T SHINK SHO.

At least Myron H. was quiet. And relatively moisture-free. This was as unbearably bad a bus ride as I had ever been on . . . and *then* we hit a pothole.

That little dental disaster was really wedged in there. We didn't get untangled until the school security guard pried her off, thinking she was a weapon of some sort.

"Wait a minute. I thought you weren't allowed to wear your helmet to school anymore."

Bah! Rules are for Vordak the Incomprehensible to *make*, not *follow*. If that cretin Combover wanted a doctor's note, a doctor's note he would have.

Principal Combover,

Vordak the Incomprehensible MUST be allowed to wear his helmet in school. This is NOT an option. It is necessary to protect his enormous brain, which, since it's so enormous, pushes against the inside of his skull. This is due to the fact that his brain is so enormous.

Sincerely,

Dr. Niarb Suomrone

Dr. Niarb Suomrone
Head of Enormous Brain Care
Enormous Brain Institute
Enormous Brain, Colorado

P.S. – He also needs the cape.

"Wait a minute—isn't Niarb Suomrone just 'enormous brain' spelled backwards?"

Pretty clever, eh? Of course Combover was totally clueless. I had that bumbling buffoon completely bamboozled. He was putty in my hands, so later that day I handed him another note.

Principal Combover,

It's me again. Vordak the Incomprehensible must also be given an additional 30 minutes at lunchtime in order to allow his brain—which, as I have already pointed out, is enormous—to cool off before his afternoon classes. I mean, he IS wearing a metal helmet around school all day, for crying out loud.

Sincerely,

Dr. Niarb Suomrone

Dr. Niarb Suomrone
Head of Enormous Brain Care
Enormous blah blah
blah de blah de blah

P.S. – He should be unsupervised during this time.

That boneheaded bumpkin bought it again! Now I had an extra half hour at lunch to spend searching for the balsoid coil. And, since things were going so well enormous-brain-note-wise, I figured it couldn't hurt to try one more.

Combover,

Furthermore, you must fork over to Vordak the Incomprehensible the sum of $100 million.

Because of that whole enormous brain thing.

Sincerely,

Vordak's Brain Guy

P.S. – Cash only.

He didn't go for it.

On Wednesday morning, I decided to give the bus one more opportunity to deliver me to school without mishap. I figured I had nothing to lose at this point and took a seat in the back of the bus, where I was immediately engulfed by the Sminion brothers, Big Vince and Little Vince.

GREAT GASSY GOBLINS! I've unearthed zombies that smelled better than those two. I made a mental note to keep the Sminions in mind for any thuggery I might require in the future.

. . . .

Later that day I had my first math quiz. As focused as I was in my search for the coil, I still had to sit through my classes in order to remain at the school. I was starting a month later than the other students but, let's face it, I am an Evil ~~Genious~~ Genius and fully capable of passing the seventh grade with nine-tenths of my brain tied behind my back. So naturally I aced the quiz. Without even studying. This stuff was a lot easier than I remembered. Unfortunately, Miss Flounmounder displayed her complete jealousy of my mathematical magnificence by grading it unfairly.

0%

Name: <u>Vordak the Incomprehensible</u>

X 1. Find the difference between the following fractions: $\dfrac{7}{16}$ $\dfrac{3}{16}$

The difference is one has a 7 on top and the other one has a 3.

X 2. Find x in the diagram below.

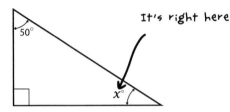

It's right here

50°

x°

X 3. Reduce the following fraction: $\dfrac{12}{64}$ $\frac{12}{64}$

X 4. Find the missing number in this sequence: 1 2 4 8 __ 32 64

It's the one between the 8 and the 32.

After a brief visit from my seven-foot-tall, four-hundred-pound attorney, Combover agreed that, technically, my answers were indeed correct. So, like I said, I aced it. And speaking of Combover, the man apparently loves the sound of his own voice because about every twenty minutes, all day long, he bombards my senses with some ridiculous announcement over the PA system.

 *"Attention. This is Principal Combover. I would like to take a moment to welcome all of our Grandparents' Day visitors and ask that you please make your way into the cafeteria. I have been told by Officer Davies that a hallway full of Farding grandparents is a fire code violation."*

. . . .

That afternoon, I returned home to find Professor Cranium hard at work on my freeze ray.

"Don't you mean your Fantastically Frigid Freeze Ray?"

Not the way Cranium was going. More like the Fantastically *Feeble* Freeze Ray. He ran his first tests on the prototype that morning and it took

him three and a half hours just to make ice cubes.
UNACCEPTABLE! Normally, I would have mocked
him right then and there, but my youthful appearance
doesn't exactly cast an intimidating shadow. So I
decided to leave Cranium a sticky note instead.

way to go, Cranium. my Darth vader
thermos keeps things colder than that,
you blundering blockhead!

- Vordak

Surely that prizewinning putdown would straighten
him out.

Thursday I had to put my search for the balsoid coil
on hold in order to deal with a **COVAFS** emergency.

"A COVAFS emergency?"

That's right—a **CO**mmander **V**irtue **A**ction **F**igure
Sighting.

"Oh, so it's an abbreviation."

No, it's an acronym. I use acronyms because they save me a lot of valuable time, at least when I don't have to explain their meaning to a yokel such as yourself. Here's another one: **Y**ou **O**bviously **K**now **E**xtremely **L**ittle.

Now, where was I before you so rudely interrupted? Ah, yes, the Commander Virtue action figure . . .

Zounds, how I despise those despicable dolls! I can't even walk past one in a store without unleashing my awesome wrath upon it!

"Maybe you're just jealous that Commander Virtue has an action figure and you don't."

Oh, I have my own action figure, all right.

At least I used to. They don't make it anymore because not enough people bought it. They *never* buy the villains—unless you can transform into a tank or an airplane or some such nonsense.

So now nothing gets my blood boiling like the sight of a kid playing with one of those vile little Virtue figures, which is exactly what some nameless little numbskull had the nerve to do in my woodworking class.

There he was, bending and twisting and flexing and contorting the repulsive little plaything into all sorts of heroic positions. Oh, how I longed to pry it from his sawdust-covered hands and stomp it into an unrecognizable blob. But I couldn't risk being suspended before I located the balsoid coil, so I quickly devised an EVIL PLAN.

VORDAK THE INCOMPREHENSIBLE'S

Foolproof Diabolical EVIL PLAN 1792

Commander Virtue Action Figure Elimination

1. Demand to use the restroom.

2. Sneak into Principal Combover's office and issue the following announcement over the PA system:

 *"All members of Mr. Thumbstump's woodworking class are to report to the nurse's station immediately for mandatory toenail-fungus inspection. This includes you, Mr. Thumbstump. Please leave all Commander Virtue action figures tied to a two-by-four on the table saw before leaving the classroom."*

3. Return to the classroom and finish off Virtue action figure.

I love it when a plan comes together.

I slept well that night. I always sleep well after successfully carrying out an EVIL PLAN. I arrived at my desk in Miss Flounmounder's math class Friday morning in a wonderful mood. Then an announcement came over the PA that changed everything.

"Attention, students. This is Principal Combover. It appears that someone vandalized the property of one of your classmates yesterday while he was being checked for toenail fungus by Nurse Belchgas. If anyone has information as to who is responsible for Craig Virtue's doll being sawed in half, please come to the office immediately. Also, Nurse Belchgas has asked that from here on out you check your own toenails for fungus."

CRAIG VIRTUE?! Could it possibly be? Could that pasty-faced little pipsqueak actually be the son of . . . COMMANDER VIRTUE?! I tracked him down in the hallway after class.

YOU, THERE. IS YOUR NAME CRAIG VIRTUE?

UH-HUH.

DOES YOUR FATHER HAPPEN TO BE . . . COMMANDER VIRTUE?

UH-HUH.

GREAT GASSY GOBLINS! THEN YOU MUST CERTAINLY KNOW WHO I AM.

SURE. YOU'RE THAT NEW KID, THE ONE WITH THE BRAIN PROBLEM, VODRAK.

IT'S VORDAK, YOU LITTLE SIM— WHAT I MEANT TO SAY WAS THAT YOUR FATHER MUST TALK ABOUT ME A LOT.

MY FATHER? NO, I DON'T THINK HE EVER MENTIONED YOU.

OH. WELL, HE PROBABLY DOESN'T LIKE TO TALK ABOUT HIS SUPERHERO WORK WHEN HE'S AT HOME, EH?

SURE HE DOES! ALL THE TIME! HE'S ALWAYS TELLING ME STORIES ABOUT HIS BATTLES WITH POWERFUL SUPERVILLAINS LIKE DR. DIABOLICAL AND MODRAX AND THE GREEN GREMLIN AND . . . THERE MUST BE HUNDREDS MORE! HE EVEN HAS PICTURES OF HIS TOP ONE HUNDRED FOES HANGING ON THE WALL OF JUSTICE IN THE FAMILY ROOM.

REALLY? AND MY HELMET STILL DOESN'T LOOK AT ALL FAMILIAR TO YOU?

WELL, NOW THAT YOU MENTION IT, THERE IS A RAKE IN THE GARAGE THAT SORT OF—

NEVER MIND!

Can you believe the nerve of that namby-pamby nincompoop, Commander Virtue? I consider *him* to be my greatest foe, my bitterest enemy, my arch-nemesis. And he doesn't even mention *me* to his son? *ME*, who has spent the better part of two decades plotting his ultimate demise? *ME*, who has captured him and placed him in my diabolically clever yet extremely slow-acting death traps no fewer than thirty-seven times? *ME*, who has rung his doorbell late at night, then run and hid in the bushes? *I* don't even merit a spot on his stupid "Wall of Justice"? That's just plain rude. It was time to revise my priorities:

VORDAK THE INCOMPREHENSIBLE'S

Remarkable Revised List of Pulse-Pounding Priorities

1. *Destroy Commander Virtue!*
2. *Destroy Commander Virtue!*
3. *Destroy Commander Virtue!*
4. Locate balsoid coil and fix Abominable Age-Reversal Ray.
5. Use Fantastically Frigid Freeze Ray to Rule the World! MUAHAHAHAHA!!!

I stayed in bed until noon that first Saturday. Who knew junior high school could be so exhausting? Without my wondrous weapons and diabolical devices, the only advantage I had over the Farding staff and students was my magnificent mind—and I was about to put it to sinister use! After getting my evil juices flowing with a quick game of Superhero Shin Kick—and eating a bowl of cinnamon Teddy Grahams, and watching six episodes of *SpongeBob SquarePants*— I set about devising a plan to dispose of Commander Virtue, an EVIL PLAN so incredibly, incomparably, inconceivably *incomprehensible* that none save Vordak himself could possibly have come up with it!

"Wow. That was a really long sentence."

Sixty words, to be precise. Each and every one of them a work of pure evil genius. I said back in the beginning of the book that I would not be "dummying" things down for you, and I meant it.

Anyway, without even trying very hard, I came up with a diabolically brilliant, foolproof EVIL PLAN to finally rid myself, and the rest of the world, of that good-for-nothing goody two-shoes. Not to brag, but this is easily in my top five diabolically brilliant, foolproof EVIL PLANS of all time. Probably number two, in fact, right behind *Refuse to Bathe Until the Entire Planet Surrenders*. And this one is going to work! And Armageddon will be much happier.

VORDAK THE INCOMPREHENSIBLE'S

Diabolically Brilliant Foolproof
EVIL PLAN 1793

Commander Virtue's Incredible Career Day Comeuppance

Step 1. Organize a Career Day at school. Parents will be invited to talk to the students about what they do for a living. There's no way that babbling blowhard will be able to pass up the opportunity to talk to kids about how wonderful he is.

Step 2. Disguise my most powerful robot as my dad.

Step 3. Schedule Dadbot to come in at the same time as Commander Virtue.

Step 4. Bring in cupcakes for the whole school.

Step 5. While Commander Virtue is speaking to the students—and thus at his most vulnerable— my Dadbot will apply a whooping of epic proportions on him. The children will be so disappointed in the pathetic Commander that they will boo him unmercifully and fling my frosted foodstuffs at his floundering form.

Step 6. Aware that he has let so many children down, the cupcake-covered Commander will slink off in shame, never to be seen or heard from again.

Step 7. Unleash Evil Laugh— MUAHAHAHAHA!!!

Step 8. Craig Virtue will probably cry. This isn't really part of the plan, but I'll enjoy it, nonetheless.

Back at the lair, Professor Cranium spent the weekend conducting his second round of experiments with the freeze-ray prototype.

"Still no 'Fantastical'?"

Hah! He'd had some success recently with the ice-cube tray, so he thought he would freeze the neighbor's pool while their kids were playing Marco Polo (okay, I have to give him *some* credit for evil creativity). Not only did the ray have no effect on the water, it actually *melted* the kids' Popsicles! I left him another note.

> Nice going, you brainless buffoon! What do you keep in that oversize head of yours, anyway — old gym socks?
>
> — Vordak

CHAPTER FOUR

Five Weeks Ago

I could scarcely believe I was starting a second week of school, and yet here I was. I had come up empty the previous week on my hunt for the balsoid coil, but, honestly, even if I located it five minutes from now, I was going to remain a student until I saw my Virtue destruction plan through. I strode defiantly into Principal Combover's office first thing Monday morning and demanded we have a Career Day. My years in Supervillainy have provided me with vast experience in demanding things, and I was not to be denied. I pounded my fist on his desk repeatedly and flailed my arms and cape about in a highly intimidating fashion. I jutted my jaw and clenched my teeth and let it be known, in no uncertain terms, that I was used to having my way. It was obvious I was someone not to be trifled with. That's when Miss Fnarbarbler, Combover's administrative assistant, came in.

EXCUSE ME, YOUNG MAN, BUT WHY ARE YOU POUNDING ON THAT DESK AND CARRYING ON THAT WAY?

WHY, TO LET PRINCIPAL COMBOVER KNOW I MEAN BUSINESS.

WELL, AS YOU CAN SEE HE'S NOT HERE. IF YOU LEAVE YOUR NAME, I'LL LET HIM KNOW YOU MEAN BUSINESS THE SECOND HE RETURNS FROM HIS MEETING. IS THERE ANYTHING I CAN HELP YOU WITH?

INDEED! I DEMAND WE HAVE A CAREER DAY HERE AT FARDING!

WELL, AREN'T YOU CUTE, WITH YOUR LITTLE HELMET AND CAPE AND GLOVES AND ALL, DEMANDING THINGS.

CUTE?! HANDSOME—
YES! STRIKING—INDEED!
STUNNING—WITHOUT
QUESTION! BUT I ABSOLUTELY,
POSITIVELY, AM NOT CUTE!

MY, YOU **ARE** PRECIOUS.

GREAT GASSY GOBLINS!
ARE WE GOING TO HAVE
A CAREER DAY OR NOT?!

ACTUALLY, WE USED TO, BUT
STOPPED A FEW YEARS AGO
AFTER AN UNFORTUNATE INCIDENT
INVOLVING A MOM WHO RAISED BOA
CONSTRICTORS. I SUPPOSE IT COULD
START UP AGAIN, BUT THAT WOULD
BE UP TO THE STUDENT COUNCIL
PRESIDENT.

AND WHO MIGHT
THAT BE?

OH, THERE ISN'T ONE.

MISS FNARBARBLER, YOU
ARE TRYING MY PATIENCE!

GOODNESS, BUT YOU'RE ADORABLE. WHAT I MEANT WAS THERE ISN'T ONE YET. THE ELECTIONS ARE IN THREE WEEKS. MARLENA LURCHBURGER IS THE OVERWHELMING FAVORITE. SHE'S A WONDERFUL YOUNG LADY. EVERYONE IN THE SCHOOL LIKES HER.

 **NOT EVERYONE.**

. . . .

I found Marlena in the cafeteria during lunch hour, surrounded by fawning classmates. I doubt Commander Virtue himself would be any more popular among the students. She actually appeared to be glowing, although that was probably just the sunlight through the windows reflecting off her perfectly white teeth. I relayed my Career Day idea, but Marlena would have no part of it. I tried to intimidate her, but the problem with being an adult Supervillain in a twelve-year-old body is no one takes you seriously when you threaten to turn their eyeballs into petroleum jelly. I found out later that Marlena's parents own and operate Wiggle's Nightcrawler and Cricket Stand in town. Apparently, she was embarrassed by the thought of them talking about their careers as bait-shop owners.

So the die was cast—if I was to have my Career Day, I, Vordak the Incomprehensible, would have to win the election and TAKE OVER THE CLASS PRESIDENCY OF FREDERICK FARDING JUNIOR HIGH SCHOOL! MUAHAHAHAHA!!! Lurchburger had already begun her election campaign. And I began mine before I left school that very day.

VOTE FOR
LURCHBURGER
FOR CLASS PRESIDENT

By that second week I had begun to notice that there was something peculiar about a couple of members of the school's staff. Well, there was something peculiar about *everybody* on the staff, but two in particular seemed especially unusual. First there is the lunch lady, Agnes Lipwartz, who, strangely enough, has a large wart on her upper lip. It's funny how many of the adults at the school have oddly descriptive last names. I just hope I'm out of here before Vice Principal Skunkbreath returns from National Guard duty. Anyway, whenever I would go through the lunch line, Lipwartz would give me much smaller portions than the other students, which was probably a good thing, particularly when the menu called for "Chef's Choice."

plop

Then there's Burfus Waxclog, the janitor. Again with the name—Waxclog suffers from tremendous amounts of waxy buildup in his ears. Whenever I walk past Waxclog, he stops whatever he is doing and watches me go by. When I am at my locker, he always seems to be busy fiddling with something nearby.

I occasionally say hello, but he never responds. I don't know whether this is because he is ignoring me or he just can't hear anything through his wax-congested ear canals. Either way, there is something about this curious custodian that's just not right. Besides the earwax thing, I mean.

· · · · · · · · · · ·

"Attention, students. This is Principal Combover. Our own Miss Chowdersox is recovering nicely and should be back at school in a few weeks. She says it's too quiet sitting at home by herself and she really misses all the noise you Farding kids make."

Speaking of sitting at home, have I mentioned how much I despise homework? It's bad enough that I'm stuck in this infernal institution for seven hours a day, but then they have the nerve to expect me to do additional work *at home*? That may be fine for the other students—I'm sure they want to learn everything they can. But I am not *them*. I am *ME*! And *ME* has too much to accomplish to waste any more time with schoolwork.

Take Mrs. Tuvier, my English teacher. She is actually substituting for Miss Chowdersox and, oddly enough, she started at Farding the same week I did. Well, one afternoon Tuvier spent fifty-five minutes discussing poetry in class, which is about fifty-four and a half minutes too many. Honestly, when am I ever going to use poetry in my everyday life? I don't know of one instance where an Evil Mastermind reached the heights of villainy through the use of rhyming verse. But did that stop Tuvier? Of course not. She droned on and on and on until my brain tissue had been reduced to cottage cheese.

And then she assigned . . . homework: *Write two poems describing yourself.* That's the real beauty of homework for teachers. It takes *them* 1.7 seconds to assign it and *you* all night to finish it. Well, I didn't have all night, so I went down to the lab and threw together yet another ingenious invention, which I named Vordak the Incomprehensible's Short-Term Rapid Rhyming Pill. One dose and, for the next sixty seconds, everything you say or write will rhyme. So, in order to get those two poems out of the way, I took one of the pills myself, and this is what I came up with:

I think that I shall never see
Another being as glorious as me.
With features so chiseled and helmet so tall,
It's no wonder that I am the envy of all.

Roses are red.
Violets are blue.
Vordak's spectacular.
How about you?

Well, that was quite simple.

Great poems, perfect timing.

But what's going on here?

My writing's still rhyming.

My rhyme pill was faulty.

Now others will scoff.

There seems to be no way

To turn my rhymes off.

No matter how greatly

I try not to rhyme,

My words come out flowery

Ev-er-y time.

And for an Arch-Villain,

Now, what could be worse

Than having your writing

All come out in verse?

I can hear Virtue laughing.

He'll find this amusing:

The uncontrolled rhyming,

The nonstop Dr. Seuss-ing.

If more ultimatums

I'm ever to send,

This poetry garbage

Must come to an end.

I've come up with a plan!

It involves the word *orange*—

There's no rhyme for THAT—

So I'm free of this . . . snorange.

Ack! That's not fair!

Now I'm making up words.

The next thing you know,

I'll say something like *shlurds*.

Well, I guess I'll admit

That my villainy's over.

Can't rule worlds like this,

So I'll keep undercover.

Hey, wait just a minute!

That last rhyme was lousy!

The pill's wearing off,

And that makes me quite . . . happy.

Needless to say, I won't be taking *that* pill again.

**"If it was needless to say, then why
did you say it?"**

Because some peabrained pains in the patoot
need to be told even those things that don't need
to be said.

"Are you talking about me?"

Does a bear live in the woods?

"Well, yeah. Where else would he stay? I mean, his paws probably can't turn a doorknob."

That was a "rhetorical" question, you muttering muttonhead. Rhetorical questions aren't meant to be answered. Do you understand?

Well, do you?

What insolence! I demand you answer me!

"Oh, I thought that was another 'rhetorical' question."

ACK! You'd best be careful, my friend. You're skating on thin ice.

"Actually, I'm sitting in my beanbag chair."

I *know* you aren't *really* skating on thin ice! That was a metaphor—you know, when you say one thing but actually mean something else!

"So, when you said I was skating on thin ice, you actually meant I was sitting in my beanbag chair?"

Of course not! I meant that you'd better be careful with the smart-alecky remarks or something unfortunate might happen to you. Got it?

"I have a Spider-Man toothbrush."

WHAT?!

"That was a metaphor. When I said, 'I have a Spiderman toothbrush,' I actually meant 'yes.'"

THAT'S NOT HOW A METAPHOR...
ZOUNDS! I hope you're proud of yourself! You just wasted an entire page and a half!

The whole bus thing hadn't worked out as I had hoped. My helmet had endured unsightly scratches and my cape carried the stench of Sminion armpit perspiration. Not to mention every time I heard the sound of the brakes, I thought Commander Virtue's propulsion boots were landing behind me. So Wednesday I drove my giant robot to school. But there was no good place to keep it.

Fortunately, Dad had kept my Roscoenator up in the attic all these years. I'd named it after my pet hamster, Roscoe. That's him on the handlebars.

Thanks to the pavement-scorching scooter's miniaturized Turbojet engine, I made it to school Thursday morning in seven seconds flat. It would have been faster, but my helmet provided a great deal of wind resistance. I must admit, the scooter looked absolutely stunning chained to the bicycle rack. And, of course, the other students simply *oozed* jealousy.

The joy I radiated from riding my remarkable Roscoenator was sucked away as soon as I took my seat in Mr. Shinetop's science class. And the joy sucker was an irritating eyesore named Benny Yoshida.

Benny was assigned to the desk next to mine, which was unfortunate, since he has some sort of nasal disorder. A greenish-yellow liquid streams down his upper lip continuously. He blows his nose at a rate of twice per minute— and he doesn't use Kleenex. His mother says it's too expensive, since he would run through five or six boxes a day. Instead, he has this horrifying handkerchief that leaves a huge wet stain in the area of his shirt pocket. Every half hour or so he wrings it out over the wastebasket.

When I first came to class, I sat three rows down from Yoshida. The second I laid eyes on that mucous-manufacturing misfit, I demanded that Shinetop require him to wear a bucket over his head at all times. Not only did he refuse my demand, he moved me right next to Benny. He claimed it was because I needed to learn to have "tolerance" for others. Once I Rule the World, Shinetop will learn to have tolerance for vats of sulfuric acid.

▪ ▪ ▪ ▪ ▪ ▪ ▪ ▪ ▪ ▪ ▪

That evening, the more I thought about Lunch Lady Lipwartz and Waxclog the janitor, the more those names seemed familiar. I decided to look back through my Scream-Inducing Scrapbook of Evil to see if anything came up. Since I was little (the first time) I've saved articles about all my evil endeavors. When I'm not feeling particularly fiendish, I pull out the scrapbook and relive my moments of misery-making mayhem. It usually perks me right up. Anyway, this is what I found:

Ah, yes. I remember that day well. That was by far the most successful of my soil-dwelling-creature weapons. (You don't even *want* to know what happened with my Miraculous Mole Beam.) It appeared that Waxclog and Lipwartz may be holding a grudge against me.

That worm-ray article got me thinking it would be best not to eat the school lunches anymore. It was probably only a matter of time before Lunch Lady Lipwartz decided to put something really unhealthy in my mashed potatoes, like rat poison or broken glass or . . . more mashed potatoes. Fortunately, Professor Cranium, although he's a lousy Evil Genius, happens to be a great cook.

*Un*fortunately, I have found that junior high school has a way of ruining pretty much everything. We have assigned seats in the cafeteria and I happen to be stuck across from Jonah Shtorp. His dad packs him a lunch *every day*—in his Commander Virtue lunch box! But that's not the worst of it. He has a tuna sandwich *every day*. Not tuna *salad*, mind you, where the tuna is all mashed up and mixed with mayonnaise, but an entire stinking, reeking, stench-emitting tuna between two pieces of bread.

When I was buying the school lunches, that sandwich didn't bother me as much. But now that I was bringing meals that actually looked, smelled, and tasted like food, I was not about to let Jonah Shtorp ruin them with his famously funky fish. Since I didn't want to spend the rest of the day in Combover's office, I let Shtorp know, as pleasantly as possible, that I would appreciate it if he brought a slightly less odoriferous sandwich for lunch from now on.

Lunch Lady Lipwartz saw what happened, threw down her serving spoon, and rushed right over. That's what I get for trying to be pleasant.

I SAW THAT, YOU LITTLE HOOLIGAN! THAT WAS A HORRIBLE THING TO DO!

WHAT? I ONLY PULLED IT OVER HIS **HEAD.** IT'S NOT LIKE HE CAN'T STILL MOVE HIS ARMS AND WALK AROUND AND STUFF. AND LOOK, I JUST FIXED IT SO HE CAN SEE WHERE HE'S GOING.

YOUNG MAN, TAKE THAT FISH OFF YOUR HEAD RIGHT THIS MINUTE.

DO I HAVE TO? THIS IS ACTUALLY PRETTY COOL.

YES, YOU HAVE TO! AND WHY DON'T YOU JUST BUY THE SCHOOL LUNCH AND AVOID THIS PROBLEM ALTOGETHER?

MY DAD WON'T LET ME EAT YOUR SCHOOL LUNCHES.

WHY NOT?

HE SAYS IT'S BECAUSE HE LOVES ME.

ALL RIGHT, THAT'S IT! GRAB BUCKETS AND MOPS, BOTH OF YOU! YOU ARE GOING TO STAY AFTER LUNCH AND SCRUB THIS FLOOR UNTIL IT'S CLEAN ENOUGH TO EAT OFF!

SO, CLEANER THAN THE PLATES?

GET MOPPING!

I made a mental note that when I Ruled the World, I would assign Lipwartz to shark-tooth-flossing duty. So, here it was—one of the lowest and highest (and lowest again) points in my recent memory. Lowest, because I, Vordak the Incomprehensible, had been reduced to mopping up crusty nacho liqui-cheese from behind a junior high school cafeteria serving counter . . . alongside a kid with a fish on his head. Highest, because I happened to glance back into the kitchen and beheld . . .

THE BALSOID COIL! It was right there attached to the back of a Clean-O-Matic dishwasher, just inside the entrance to the kitchen. I could almost taste it, although that might just have been tuna juice left on my fingers from earlier. Lowest again, because the doorway was blocked by an iron gate that was kept locked except during lunch period— and Lunch Lady Lipwartz had the only key.

The excitement over my recent discovery kept me up late Friday night. But there would be no sleeping late *this* weekend. I had an election to plan. I had a balsoid coil to swipe. And, by a magnificent stroke of luck, the science fair was a week from this coming Thursday. I was just going to enter a death ray or a propulsion boot or something else I had lying around, but with my recent discovery of the balsoid coil, I have come up with a diabolical plan to both win first prize *and* retrieve the elusive coil from the clutches of Lipwartz.

VORDAK THE INCOMPREHENSIBLE'S

Diabolical EVIL PLAN 1794

Seriously Sinister Science-Fair Scheme

Step 1. Create a Magnificent Matter Transporter and enter it in the fair.

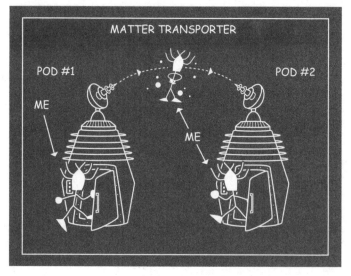

Step 2. After winning first place, alter one of the pods to look like a refrigerator.

Step 3. When taking down science-fair project, leave the altered pod near the door to the kitchen. Mistaking it for a real refrigerator, Lunch Lady Lipwartz will have it moved into the kitchen, next to the dishwasher.

Step 4. Transport myself from the other pod, which is now back in my lair, to the pod in the kitchen.

Step 5. Disconnect the balsoid coil from the dishwasher and bring it with me when I transport myself back to my lair.

Step 6. Send Lipwartz the following letter:

Dear Lunch Lady Lipwartz,

PPHHHFFFFFTTTTT!!

— Vordak

Step 7. Unleash Evil Laugh—
MUAHAHAHAHA!!!

All those wearisome water-cycle diagrams and unbearable baking-soda volcanoes would pale before the science-fair superiority of my triumphant transporter! Ah, devising this particularly pleasing Evil Plan put me in such a good mood that I decided to give my henchmen a treat and took them on a picnic.

If I was to defeat Lurchburger and win the class presidency, I had to begin in earnest. So many Evil Plans, so little time! I was going to need some help, so I invited my four closest and most trusted classmates over on Sunday to discuss positions on my election campaign staff.

 I MUST TELL YOU, MYRON H., THAT I PREFER TO CALL PEOPLE BY THEIR LAST NAMES. THIS ALLOWS ME TO AVOID DEVELOPING ANY PERSONAL CONNECTIONS WITH IGNORAMUSES THAT I AM VASTLY SUPERIOR TO. WHAT DOES THE H STAND FOR?

NOTHING.

 WELL, IT CAN'T STAND FOR NOTHING. YOUR LAST NAME CERTAINLY ISN'T H.

ACTUALLY, IT'S PRONOUNCED "H-PERIOD."

DO YOU MEAN TO TELL ME YOUR NAME IS MYRON H-PERIOD? WHY, THAT'S PREPOSTEROUS!

IT USED TO BE HREBOWNIFLAPISTANEWICZ, BUT MY MOM COULDN'T FIT IT ON MY UNDERWEAR WAISTBANDS.

YOUR MOM LEGALLY CHANGED YOUR NAME BECAUSE IT WAS TOO LONG FOR YOUR UNDERWEAR?

I HAVE A SANDWICH BAG FILLED WITH CARROT STICKS IN MY BACKPACK.

WHAT DOES THAT HAVE TO DO WITH IT?

NOTHING. I JUST WANTED TO CHANGE THE SUBJECT.

H-Period had already proven to excel at nametag creation, and his position as president of the Color Copier Club would be a big help with poster production. I made him my Minion in Charge of Promotion.

Fara Farkesh, as it turns out, is the smartest student in the entire school. Aside from me. She doesn't get the best grades, but that's mostly because her dental apparatus tends to ruin her schoolwork.

ITSH SHO NISHE TO SHEE YOU AGAIN, VORDAK! I'M SHUPER SHTOKED TO ASHISHT YOU. I CAN SHINK OF SHIX OR SHEVEN SHINGSH TO—

ALL RIGHT, JUST STOP, ALREADY!

SHTOP?

YESH! I MEAN YES! I HAVE NEED OF YOUR TALENTS, BUT YOUR SPITTLE-SPEWING SPEECH IS BEGINNING TO RUST MY HELMET. FROM NOW ON, YOU MUST AVOID USING THE LETTER S WHEN SPEAKING TO ME.

LET ME SHINK THAT SHROUGH. I'M OK WISH IT IF YOU SHINK IT WILL HELP.

ACK! NO TH'S, EITHER!

VERY WELL. I'LL TRY. WHAT CAN I DO TO HELP? I'M A REALLY GOOD WRITER AND I LOVE TO READ AND I CAN DRAW A LITTLE BIT AND I BAKE A MEAN OATMEAL COOKIE AND I PLAY WONDERFUL TROMBONE AND I'M A DEBATE CLUB MEMBER AND I PLAY VOLLEYBALL AND I—

STOP! I THOUGHT YOU COULD HELP WRITE MY SPEECH.

OKAY. YEAH. UH-HUH. I'D BE DELIGHTED TO. IT WOULD BE AN HONOR. CAN'T WAIT TO GET GOING. I'LL GET RIGHT ON IT. I WANT TO—

GREAT GASSY GOBLINS . . .

It appeared as though I had stemmed the flow of Farkesh's saliva, if not her words. That left the Sminion brothers, Big Vince and Little Vince. I didn't get the feeling the Vinces' parents were the sharpest needles in the laboratory, if you catch my drift.

 BIG VINCE, I AM ALLOWING YOU AND YOUR BROTHER THE GREAT PRIVILEGE TO SERVE AS MY SECURITY WHEN I'M AT SCHOOL.

I'M LITTLE VINCE.

 BUT YOU'RE BIGGER THAN YOUR BROTHER.

OLDER, TOO.

 ACK! THEN WHY IS BIG VINCE YOUR BROTHER?

 BECAUSE WE HAVE THE SAME PARENTS. DON'T YOU KNOW HOW THAT WORKS?

OF COURSE I KNOW HOW IT WORKS! WHY DID YOUR PARENTS NAME YOU BOTH VINCE?!

 IT WAS THEIR FAVORITE NAME. CAN WE GO NOW? I HAVE TO GET HOME AND FEED VINCE.

 HE CAN'T FEED HIMSELF?

OF COURSE NOT.
HE'S A TURTLE.

BIG VINCE IS A . . .
TURTLE?

AND I THOUGHT I
WASN'T VERY BRIGHT. BIG
VINCE IS A PERSON, VODRAK.
VINCE IS A TURTLE.

IT'S VORDAK! AND WHY BY THE
FROZEN MOONS OF HARVAT DID
YOU NAME YOUR TURTLE VINCE?

BECAUSE IF WE DIDN'T,
WE WOULDN'T KNOW
WHAT TO CALL HIM.

WELL, WHAT ABOUT
FRED?

WHO'S FRED?

YOUR TURTLE!

I THINK YOU'RE
CONFUSED, VODRAK. MY
TURTLE IS VINCE.

 **IT'S VORDAK!!**

 *NO, I'M POSITIVE IT'S VINCE. YOU'RE VORDAK.*

I sent them all home and took out my frustration with a little exercise.

SLAM!

CHAPTER FIVE

Four Weeks Ago

I put together a three-pronged ~~attack~~ campaign strategy for winning the Farding Junior High presidential election, which I decided to call:

VORDAK THE INCOMPREHENSIBLE'S

Three-Pronged ~~Attack~~ Campaign Strategy
for Winning the Farding Junior High
Presidential Election

Prong 1. Make Marlena Lurchburger look bad.

Prong 2. Make Vordak the Incomprehensible
look good.
Prong 3. Cheat.

I usually prefer six or seven prongs in my strategies, but this would have to do. Besides, I still had prong three, which is a staple of any Vordak the Incomprehensible strategy. Zounds, I love saying "prong"!

With the election less than three weeks away, I would have to kick my scheming into high gear. But I would have to do it with the stench of failure hanging over my handsome head because, in what was surely one of the rarest events in the history of mankind, I, Vordak the Incomprehensible, was forced to admit defeat. I have commanded vast armies of minions. I have created giant, orbiting space lairs. I have caused world leaders to openly sob while listening to my unthinkable ultimatums! But I could not find a good way to get to and from school—even though, as is always the case, it was through absolutely no fault of my own.

I had been riding the Roscoenator, which had been working out pretty well. However, as I approached the bicycle rack after school that Monday, I discovered that some pint-size plunderer had tried to steal it! Luckily, the scooter's security system foiled the attempted theft.

But who knows if I would be as fortunate the next time? The mere thought of the ravishing Roscoenator in the hands of some scooter-snatching scoundrel made me sick to my stomach . . . although that could just have been the thirteen chocolate Pop-Tarts I had for breakfast—or the chocolate milk shake I washed them down with.

So Tuesday I decided to walk to school. And I calculated that I could knock fifteen minutes off my travel time by cutting through Mrs. Brundlefly's yard. There's a short fence separating our properties, but I was able to negotiate that with little problem.

Of course, the next morning I stepped into my backyard to find this:

Sure, I may have trampled her roses and knocked over her garbage cans, but it's not like I did those things on purpose. Well, all right, the garbage cans were on purpose. I've just never been able to walk past one of those reeking rubbish receptacles without tipping it over and spewing its contents all over the place. That's just how I roll. And it's possible the rose trampling might also have been somewhat intentional. I mean, they were sitting right there in front of me, for Kromnar's sake—I hardly even had to veer.

No matter. I solved this new problem, as well.

I arrived at school ready to launch the first prong of my election campaign: *make Marlena Lurchburger look bad in the eyes of the voters.* The easiest way to do that would be to blast her with a few rounds of my handheld ugly ray, but I wasn't able to get it past the school's security checkpoint.

So, what other options did I have to make her popularity take a nosedive? One of my old favorites— *lying*! Making up stories that leave the victim looking like an ignoramus of the highest degree. Like when I placed an ad in the *Chronicle* that claimed Commander Virtue stuck rolled-up gym socks in his costume sleeves to make his muscles appear larger. Well, that actually turned out to be true, but I didn't know it at the time. The important thing was that my comment made him look like a legendary lamebrain, at least for a little while.

I decided to let my campaign minions handle the lies. It was best if none of this could be traced directly back to me—at least until after the election. The problem was they're terrible liars, especially Myron H., and I didn't have time to follow them around all day long telling them what ridiculous rumors to spread. I needed to create some sort of mind-bogglingly bold bald-faced-lie generator that they could carry around with them. So I did.

VORDAK THE INCOMPREHENSIBLE'S

Mind-Bogglingly Bold Bald-Faced-Lie Generator

Instructions:
1. Choose the name of the imbecile you wish to lie about.
2. Select a three-digit number.
3. Fill in the blanks using the columns below.

Did you hear about _____(name)_____ **?**

He/She _____(1)_____ **a(n)** _____(2)_____

for _____(3)_____ **!**

Example: Marlena Lurchburger, 251
"Did you hear about Marlena Lurchburger?
She licked a janitor's mop for a dollar!"

Digit (1)	Digit (2)	Digit (3)
0 spit on	0 science-lab frog	0 a good twenty minutes
1 sniffed	1 scab	1 a dollar
2 licked	2 armpit stain	2 kicks
3 sat on	3 lunchroom hot dog	3 no good reason
4 stared at	4 exchange student	4 looking at him/her funny
5 kissed	5 janitor's mop	5 Leif Eriksson Day
6 screamed at	6 wet gym shoe	6 the third time this week
7 sang to	7 volleyball	7 a chance to win a toaster
8 snuggled	8 pimple	8 making him/her angry
9 slapped	9 naked mole rat	9 good luck

And there you go! Sometimes I even amaze myself. Like right now. And now. And again . . . . . . *now*! I can only imagine how often I must amaze *you*. Feel free to use the Lie Generator yourself—it's included with the price of the book.

"Did you hear about Vordak the Incomprehensible? He—"

GIVE ME THAT!!!

. . . .

After a brief tutoring session, I unleashed Farkesh and the Sminions to spread their fiendish falsehoods throughout the school. Meanwhile, Myron H. and I began work on campaign posters.

Of course, we also had to take care of the posters Marlena was putting up all over the school.

Hey, they can't all be gems

As it turns out, the Sminion brothers were not as effective as I had hoped at using my Bald-Faced-Lie Generator. Big Vince reads at a second-grade level and Little Vince couldn't come up with any three-digit numbers. And holding a piece of paper upside down while mumbling and scratching your head isn't a very effective way to drum up voter support. Working to their strengths, though, I found other ways for the gargantuan galoots to "sway" voters.

Mrs. Brundlefly had been keeping herself quite busy while I was in school. When I returned home Wednesday, I found:

Did this woeful woman not realize who she was dealing with? Was she really attempting to match wits with one of the truly extraordinary, not to mention handsome, Evil Masterminds of all time? Needless to say, the next morning I took the shortcut as usual because, thanks to my criminal craftiness, I had once again proven myself superior to Mrs. Brundlefly!

Even so, she was becoming a royal pain in my backside. I have battled many a Superhero with far less resolve than this grizzled old gal. Nevertheless, this latest display of my unimaginable power would surely leave her thinking twice about thwarting the will of Vordak the Incomprehensible!

Then again, maybe not.

So, now it was taking me half an hour to walk to school thanks to Mrs. Brundlefly's impenetrable barrier, which put me in a foul mood before I even *arrived* at school that Friday. And then Benny Yoshida's desk collapsed during science class, probably due to the added weight of all the snot smeared on it. Anyway, Waxclog said it would take a week or so to dig another desk out of the basement. He also made a suggestion to Shinetop about what to do in the meantime.

Any doubt was now erased—this was definitely the same Burfus Waxclog whose apartment I flooded with earthworms.

That afternoon in gym class, Coach Whistlespit announced that we would be playing hockey. Fantastic! A chance to take out my frustrations with the carefree clobbering of my classmates! I could hardly contain myself. And then he brought out the "equipment."

Foam? Boy, have things changed. It used to be an evil kid could count on gym class as an opportunity to harass and bully the smaller, weaker, less intimidating students. And not even get in trouble for it! Why, dodgeball alone would keep the school nurse busy all afternoon. But with this equipment? I spent the entire forty-five minutes whacking away at the back of Melvin Tinkler's knees. And what did I get for all my effort? Nothing. Not so much as a sniffle. And Melvin cries if his *gloves* are too tight. I had a better chance of witnessing an injury in my English class.

The weekend arrived and, sadly, so did another failed test for Professor Cranium and his famously faulty freeze ray. You know, when you come up with your EVIL PLAN for world domination, you naturally assume that the bloat-headed super-intellectual brainy ~~genious~~ genius guy you hired will be able to create whatever type of ray you call for. That *is* their main purpose, after all. I certainly didn't bring Professor Cranium aboard because he's good at checkers— which, by the way, he isn't.

I don't even know what he tried to freeze this time around, but the minute I entered his laboratory, I knew he had botched it again.

Yes, that is correct. I said "his" laboratory. I built a state-of-the-art, fully equipped Evil Laboratory for a brilliant Evil "Scientist" whose freeze ray *melts* Popsicles. Who knew? Clearly, it was time for another note.

You inept imbecile, Cranium! I've scraped organisms smarter than you off the bottom of my boots! And the stick I used to do the scraping was also smarter than you!
Little Vince Sminion would make a better scientist!

— Vordak

P.S. — Are we still on for lunch tomorrow?

CHAPTER SIX

Three Weeks Ago

I was having a hard time concentrating in my classes. The teachers droned on day after day about pronouns or hypotenuses or photosynthesis. And do you think they could hold my attention? Of course not! What is some run-of-the-mill science instructor going to teach me, Vordak the Incomprehensible, about the reproductive system of a frog that I don't already know from my experiments to create an army of giant octotoads? I found it increasingly difficult to keep my mind from wandering.

What's worse, the teachers were all jealous of me. How else to explain the mediocre grades I was receiving? You remember Mrs. Tuvier, my English teacher? Well, she is one of those annoyingly positive, optimistic, smiley people who wouldn't know a piece of creative writing if it jumped up and bit her on the nose. (And, yes, I have Cranium working on a type of paper that would do exactly that.)

A few days ago, I was handed back my first graded essay. Here was the assignment:

Describe the person sitting next to you.
What is it about that person that makes them unique and special?

Ronald Penobscot

by VORDAK THE INCOMPREHENSIBLE

Ronald Penobscot is a young human male. He looks fairly healthy, but his ears are larger than normal. Kind of like two pieces of bologna stapled to the side of his head. Ronald is wearing brown shoes.

The End

C–

Vordak – This is a bit short. Talk about what he is like on the inside as well as the outside.

You see what I'm talking about? A C-minus? Preposterous! So, instead of basking in the praise this essay so richly deserved, I spent that night rewriting an already perfect paper and handed it back in the following day.

Ronald Penobscot

by VORDAK THE INCOMPREHENSIBLE

Ronald Penobscot is a young human male. He looks fairly healthy, but his ears are larger than normal. Kind of like two pieces of bologna stapled to the side of his head. Ronald is wearing brown shoes. I can't see his insides without my X-ray visor but, based on the sounds I hear coming from his direction during class, I assume he has a bowel problem.

The End

C

Vordak - Not bad, but try to use more positive words like exceptional and outstanding.

This latest effort should have received, at the very least, a standing ovation. From the entire school district. Tuvier obviously thought she could defeat me, but I vowed not to stop until I received the grade I so richly deserved! I spent yet another evening revising, with *breathtaking* results!

Ronald Penobscot

by VORDAK THE INCOMPREHENSIBLE

Ronald Penobscot sits next to Vordak the Incomprehensible. He is
exceptional and outstanding. And by "he" I mean me, Vordak the
Incomprehensible. I am the envy of all the other students, blessed
with unsurpassed leadership abilities and stunning good looks. I am
head and shoulders above anything else this planet has to offer, truly
remarkable in every way, and it is only a matter of time before I take
my rightful place as RULER OF THE WORLD! MUAHAHAHAHA!!!
He is wearing brown shoes. And by "he" I mean Ronald.

The End.

C+

*Vordak - Better. Nice use of exceptional and
outstanding.*

A C-plus! YES! Once again I have achieved the
impossible! MUAHAHAHAHA!!!

"Attention, students. This is Principal Combover. I have received complaints from the crossing guards that, at the end of the day, a number of students leave Farding and don't stop when they are instructed to. We will be adding additional crossing guards in an effort to control these Farding students. If you are interested in helping out, please see Coach Whistlespit."

. . . .

With the election scheduled for the following week, it was time to get started on the second prong of my election campaign—*make Vordak the Incomprehensible look good.* Now, I know what you're thinking*.

"What?"

I said, "I know what you're thinking." *

"And I said, 'What?'"

---

* You respond by saying, "That you're so good looking already, what more could you possibly do?"

ACK! Do you not see the asterisk after the word *thinking*?

"Yeah, I see it. Why?"

Great Gassy Goblins! Don't you know how asterisks work?! Look at the footnote at the bottom of the previous page and see what it means!

**"Okay. Hold on a second. Ah. Got it.
That you're so good looking . . ."**

Hold on! I need to start over again or none of this will make any sense. Are you ready?

"Yeppers."

All right, here we go. It was time to get started on the second prong of my election campaign—*make Vordak the Incomprehensible look good.* Now, I know what you're thinking*.

**"That you're so good looking already,
what more could you possibly do?"**

Exactly.

ACK! It's what EVERYONE was thinking, you deranged doofus! Sure, simply by showing up at school every day I was giving voters an eyeful of my hands-down, high-end handsomeness. But I needed to do more to interact with the students, to let them get to know me outside the classroom. And this crossing-guard thing was just the ticket.

I began my tour of duty at four o'clock that afternoon.

I was relieved of duty by Coach Whistlespit promptly at 4:02. I didn't have the opportunity to meet many kids, but I am proud to say I set the record for the shortest time anyone has held the position in the forty-seven-year history of the school!

Benny Yoshida arrived at our desk Tuesday with a cold. Amazingly, this resulted in an even higher level of nasal discharge than usual. What's worse, it also resulted in occasional sneezing.

Shockingly, Waxclog still hadn't delivered Benny's new desk. Well, enough was enough! I decided to take matters into my own hands and brought something in for show-and-tell the next day.

ROCKETS! Perhaps I hadn't given this school a fair chance. Any educational institution with its own space program couldn't be *all* bad. And this provided an excellent opportunity to interact with student voters who shared my interest in interplanetary travel. Since this was the first meeting of the year, I figured we would be limited to an orbit or two around the earth, so I brought one of my smaller rockets.

I was shocked to find that none of the other astronauts were outfitted for a journey into space. And how in Yorvath's name were they going to fit inside those tiny little spacecrafts? I asked Shinetop what kind of sorry space program he was running.

He said this was a *model* rocket club and that most of the rockets reached a height of about three hundred feet. Three hundred feet? Last I checked, there were no planets within three hundred feet of the earth's surface. ACK! With Shinetop heading the program, not only would we not be orbiting the earth or any other planetary object, I wasn't even allowed to man my rocket. I decided to save fuel and just shut the launch down altogether. It was just as well, I suppose—the science fair was tomorrow and I had some last-minute adjustments to make on my matter-transporter pods.

VALUABLE BONUS INFORMATION!

All right, I've decided to take a brief break from the telling of my intriguing tale in order to give you a valuable piece of bonus information. I have no idea why I would do something like this, but you should consider yourself extremely fortunate because you certainly don't deserve it. Anyway, without further ado, I present you with . . .

VORDAK THE INCOMPREHENSIBLE'S

SUREFIRE WAY TO GET BETTER GRADES ON TESTS

1. Volunteer to collect the completed exams and bring them to the teacher's desk.

2. Before you hand them in, use your belt-buckle-mounted heat beam to incinerate everyone's test except for yours and Donald Lubener's, who has not once in his academic career achieved a grade above D-.

3. Convince the teacher to grade on a curve.

NOTE: This technique only works if you have Donald Lubener in your class AND you are smarter than he is.

The day of the science fair had finally arrived, and what a thoroughly thrilling Thursday it was! My main objective, of course, was to use my Miraculous Matter Transporter to nab the balsoid coil from Lipwartz's fortified kitchen. But I also HAD TO HAVE that first-place ribbon! *If there is an award to be won, Vordak the Incomprehensible shall win it!* That's a motto of mine, along with *Nothing conquered, nothing gained* and *You can rearrange the letters in COMMANDER VIRTUE to get CRUDE VOMITER MAN.*

That morning, we all set up our display boards in the gymnasium, but some of the students were waiting until the start of the fair that evening to bring in their actual projects. I originally thought winning that ribbon would be a cinch, but it was looking like I might have some real competition.

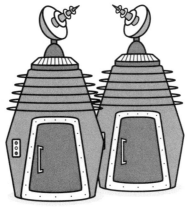

Vortex generators? Hovercrafts? I may have underestimated my adolescent adversaries. How are twelve-year olds even capable of such feats of genius? Other than me, I mean. I'll bet they had help from their parents.

. . . .

"Attention, students. This is Principal Combover. I would like to remind you that there are still plenty of openings to make beautiful music as a member of our very own Farding band. If you're interested, stop by the music room after school today."

Since my exhibit was set up and ready to go, I had some free time at the end of the day. My excitement was building and I needed something to pass the time before the start of the fair. I decided to impress my fellow students, and voters, by treating their grateful ears to a sampling of my legendary musical prowess. I dropped by the music room and, after a thorough evaluation of my musical ability, was given an instrument that "matched my skill level."

As if that wasn't bad enough, they stuck me in the brass section, which presented a couple of real problems—Curtis Clef and Stephen Sharp.

How could a musician with my obvious gifts be expected to fully display his immense talent while having to deal with these decidedly distracting dimwits? Luckily, Security Minion Little Vince Sminion was in the room (he plays the piccolo) and helped solve both problems quickly and efficiently, although it may have cost me a couple votes.

The science fair that evening was an opportunity for everyone to witness my true brilliance, so long as the other projects didn't outshine my own magnificent matter transporter. I was particularly worried about the vortex generator—powerful, roaring funnels of nearly unimaginable destructive energy tend to be real crowd pleasers. I had a backup plan ready just in case. It consisted of my hand, the fire alarm, and a firm, crisp pulling motion. As it turned out, I had no need to worry.

The hovercraft was cobbled together from a pie tin, a straw, and a balloon. And the vortex generator consisted of two two-liter soda bottles taped together and filled with colored water. That first-place ribbon was as good as mine! MUAHAHAHAHA!!!

After an hour or so of demonstrating my tyrannical transporter, I decided to stroll around and check out the other exhibits. Who knows, I might discover a future super-intellectual to bring into my organization and replace Professor Cranium. Someone capable of designing brilliantly evil weapons and diabolically clever yet extremely slow-acting Superhero death traps. No such luck, unless my plans to conquer the planet included a miniature papier-mâché mountain that spewed vinegar and baking soda. There was one interesting display involving a large magnet, but I was quickly reminded of why I seldom use magnetism in my own sinister schemes.

I returned to my own project to find the prizes had been awarded.

VORTEX GENERATOR

RUNNER-UP

GREAT GASSY GOBLINS! That was totally unfair! The first thing I'm going to do once I Rule the World is teleport all junior high schools to Venus. First prize actually went to Myron H., but his award came under the condition that he promise never to open his project on school property.

After cooling off a bit, I did what was necessary for EVIL PLAN 1794 by altering one of the transporter pods to resemble a refrigerator and moving it near the entrance to the kitchen.

I also altered the science-fair awards to more accurately reflect their worth.

Friday at lunch, I noticed that my disguised matter-transportation pod had indeed been moved into the kitchen, next to the dishwasher, which had the coil on the back. YES! Another of Vordak the Incomprehensible's diabolical EVIL PLANS was coming together! MUAHAHAHAHA!!!

I had the Vinces take the other pod to my lair so that, when the time came, everything was set for me to transport myself to the school, grab the coil, and transport back. But I had to be patient. There was still Commander Virtue to dispose of, and that could only happen once I became class president and organized Career Day.

The election was only a week away, and I still had

plenty to do. My attempts to socialize with the other students in order to better let them experience my immense glory had not gone as well as I had hoped. I needed something bigger. I needed something where more eyes could be upon me. I needed an announcement from Combover.

"Attention, students. This is Principal Combover. Just a reminder that we have a home basketball game tonight against our archrival, Doss. Let's really pack the stands and let those Owls know just how loud a gymnasium full of Farding Ferrets can be!"

An entire gym filled with voters! This was the opportunity I had been waiting for. I wasn't sure what I was going to do, but I sent word for my campaign minions to meet me after school at the game.

As it turned out, the Doss bus broke down on the way to the game and they arrived an hour late. I didn't have time to go home and come back again, so I sat there and watched the entertainment, which consisted of Jonah Shtorp running around in a giant ferret costume.

Which gave me yet another brilliant idea. Just before halftime, Shtorp left to use the bathroom. I dispatched Little Vince to "borrow" the head from him while Big Vince came up with the most efficient design possible for a five-person pyramid. Apparently, Shtorp was still wearing the fish on his noggin because it smelled like a baked-bean factory's port-a-john inside that ferret head. But Supervillainy requires true dedication, so I took a deep breath, donned the costume, and joined my minions at center court.

The good news is the whole thing went off without a hitch. Well, other than the collapsed abdomen suffered by Myron H. The bad news is nobody saw us, because a glowing Marlena Lurchburger was handing out free candy and "Vote for Marlena" buttons in the far corner of the gym.

CHAPTER SEVEN

Two Weeks Ago

Monday morning started off a bit slowly. Apparently my run-in with the magnet during the science fair had a few lingering effects.

Who even knew Coach Whistlespit had a metal plate in his head? Luckily, I remembered reading on the science-project board that striking an object sharply can demagnetize it. So, after prying the helmet clean of metal objects, I had Myron H. put it on and run into the wall a few hundred times.

KLANG

The election was Friday and I was into the final phase of the second prong of my strategy—*make Vordak the Incomprehensible look good.* I figured I still needed one big event to set me up perfectly to defeat Lurchburger. I spent the remainder of Monday and Tuesday just going through the motions in my classes, waiting impatiently for Combover to provide me with another opportunity to showcase my amazingosity.

 "Attention, students. This is Principal Combover. As you know, the school play, Pirates of the Caribbean, will be held tomorrow evening in the cafeteria. As an added treat, the choir will be performing its Farding rendition of 'Oh! Susanna' during the intermission. I hope to see you all there along with your families."

And there it was! Now, I had never acted in a play, because the thought of spending time as someone other than Vordak the Incomprehensible, even for a short while, seemed unbearable. But I needed the votes, and I knew that with one look at me in the spotlight, the audience would be smitten. So I went to see Miss Purdy, the play's director, after school.

 I DEMAND TO KNOW MORE ABOUT THE PLAY YOU'RE PUTTING ON TOMORROW EVENING!

WELL, WE'LL BE PERFORMING THE MUSICAL VERSION OF **PIRATES OF THE CARIBBEAN**. YOU SHOULD COME. I THINK YOU'LL REALLY ENJOY IT. BY THE WAY, CONSIDERATE STUDENTS DON'T DEMAND THINGS— THEY ASK POLITELY.

I'M SURE THEY DO. NOW, I DEMAND TO PLAY THE ROLE OF JACK SPARROW. I REQUIRE A SCRIPT IMMEDIATELY SO I CAN BEGIN GOING OVER MY LINES!

I'M SORRY, BUT THE CAST AND CREW HAVE BEEN REHEARSING FOR THE PAST THREE WEEKS AND ALL THE ROLES HAVE BEEN FILLED. CRAIG VIRTUE WILL BE PLAYING JACK SPARROW.

WHAT?! I HAVE MORE ACTING TALENT IN MY LEFT BOOT THAN THAT SORRY SON OF A SUPERHERO HAS IN HIS ENTIRE MISERABLE BODY!

WELL, ALL THE MAIN ROLES ARE ALREADY FILLED, BUT I CERTAINLY WOULD HATE TO TURN AWAY ANY INTERESTED STUDENT. I'LL TELL YOU WHAT—BE HERE AN HOUR EARLY TOMORROW NIGHT AND I'LL COME UP WITH A SPECIAL PART FOR YOU TO PLAY. BY THE WAY, CONSIDERATE STUDENTS DON'T CALL OTHER STUDENTS NAMES.

I'M SURE THEY DON'T, BUT THAT'S BECAUSE THEY'RE IMBECILES.

So, a SPECIAL part! It appeared Miss Purdy had an eye for talent, after all.

Well, pea-brained Purdy didn't put quite as much effort into creating my role as I had expected.

When I first arrived, I overheard Combover and Purdy talking. Combover was nervous about me being in the play, but Purdy assured him there was no way I could do any harm with the role she gave me. I love a challenge!

I wasn't invited to take a bow during the curtain call.

Election day was here at last! And I was getting that warm, fuzzy feeling I had whenever I was about to conquer something. My part in the play had hardly been memorable, but the sinking of the pirate ship had certainly seared me into the minds of everyone in attendance. Lurchburger and I would give our speeches during an assembly at 11:00 a.m. Imagine, a mere girl of twelve attempting to match the oratory onslaught of Vordak the Incomprehensible! I, who have issued ultimatums to kings! I, who have threatened entire continents over the television airwaves. I, who once spent over two hours revealing to Commander Virtue, while he was groaning in the grisly grasp of yet another of my diabolically clever yet extremely slow-acting death traps, the details of my EVIL PLAN to make all the world's escalators run only in the downward direction. Sure, he went on to escape and thwart my EVIL PLAN, but that's beside the point. I can give a heck of a speech!

I had no doubt I could win the election fair and square. I also had no doubt that "fair and square" is a concept that no self-respecting Supervillain would ever be caught abiding by. So I went to prong three of my campaign strategy (cheating) and, when she wasn't looking, I snatched Lurchburger's speech from her backpack, made a minor change, and slipped it back in.

Welcome fellow students of Frederick Farding Junior High School. I ~~will be~~ **wear boys'** *brief~~s~~*

If elected your Class President, I will strive to do the very best job I possibly can. I promise

I~~f~~ ⸻ ⸻ Presid⸻

After the speeches, the students would vote and I would be ~~coronated~~ named class president promptly at 3:00, at which time I would allow student and teacher groveling to begin. But first I had to sit through art class, where it was "Popsicle stick" day. Miss Purdy, who also happens to be the art teacher, instructed us to create something

imaginative by gluing Popsicle sticks together and then painting our creations in an artistic manner. Most of the kids made either picture frames or coasters. For the last fifty years most kids have made either picture frames or coasters. And they never get any better.

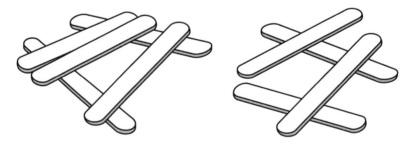

How this can be classified as "art" is beyond me. I refused to be dragged down to the loathsome level of my talentless classmates. If I was to spend an entire hour creating a work of art, the subject must be worthy of my talent and effort. And there is only one such subject in existence!

Eleven o'clock arrived and Marlena Lurchburger did not disappoint—*me*! She read her speech, complete with my little revision. I don't think she realized what she had said because she didn't even flinch.

Then came my turn—time to finish Lurchburger off with a brilliant, rousing, epic speech to my future underlings. My wondrous words would without doubt win the day. I gathered a deep breath and unleashed my awe-inspiring address.

Greetings, you sorry sack of simpletons. Let me get right to the point. Leaders are chosen because they are smarter, stronger, and better looking than those they will lead. Does that sound like Marlena Lurchburger to you? Of course not! It sounds like me, Vordak the Incomprehensible! Therefore, I am the obvious choice to become your Supreme Ruler— err, class president. Now, those of you who can operate a pencil— vote quickly! I have much yet to accomplish! MUAHAHAHAHA!!!

Yes, it sounded as magnificent in person as it does reading it here. In fact, it brings a tear to my eye just thinking about it. Now it was just a matter of waiting until three o'clock for the countdown to the destruction of Commander Virtue to begin!

. . . .

Marlena won. Even in the retelling of this story I can scarcely believe it. Apparently, *most* of the girls at Farding wear boys' briefs. So do a lot of the boys. So they all voted for her. In fact, I only received thirty-five votes—four from my campaign team, thirty from me (that's all I had time to fill out), and one from that kid with the fish on his head. Apparently he really likes it. As runner-up, I was given the position of *vice president*. Imagine, Vordak the Incomprehensible—Malevolent Master of Evil—second in command to a seventh grader! So long, Career Day. Good-bye, demise of Commander Virtue. In all my years of Supervillainy I had never been this depressed and downtrodden. I had lost my best chance to dispose of my arch-nemesis and I would likely never feel joy again.

The End

*"Wait a minute! Back in the beginning of the book
you were sitting there all happy and confident
and stuff waiting for Commander Virtue
to make his Career Day speech."*

And?

*"And I paid for the book
so I want to hear the rest of the story!"*

Really.

"Yes, REALLY!"

Then ask politely.

"Will you PLEASE tell the rest of your story?"

MORE politely.

*"Will you PRETTY PRETTY PRETTY PLEASE
tell the rest of your story?"*

That was pathetic. Let me give you a bit of advice—
if you ever hope to Rule the World yourself, you can't
go around being all wimpy and polite like that. Have
you ever heard ME be polite?

"No. But you've never Ruled the World, either."

BUT I SOON SHALL! And that little remark just reserved you a spot at the front of the piranha-tank line! Now, grab a pen and paper and write "I am undeserving of the pleasure of reading Vordak's remarkable writings" fifty thousand times. Come back when you finish and I will continue the story.

CHAPTER EIGHT

One Week Ago

As it turns out, there is a little-known rule that says the class vice president (ME!) takes over as class president if the current president acts in a manner unbefitting the position.

Well, who (ME!) would have thought that keeping a family of rabid weasels in your locker would be considered an act unbefitting the position of president?

And who (ME!) would have put them there in the first place?

And just who on earth (Myron H.—but I told him

to do it!) would have slipped a note under Principal Combover's door telling him to look in Lurchburger's locker?

Lurchburger was out and I was in! THE CLASS PRESIDENCY OF FREDERICK FARDING JUNIOR HIGH SCHOOL WAS MINE! MUAHAHAHAHA!!!

I couldn't wait to begin flaunting my newfound power, so the next day I delivered the following letter to Combover:

Principal Combover,

Now that I have risen to the Office of the Presidency, I feel a few changes are in order. Don't worry, your position as principal will not be affected...for the time being. I do, however, expect the following to be completed by the end of the week:

- A statue of myself shall be erected at the entrance to the school.

- The name of the school will officially be changed to **THE VORDAK T. INCOMPREHENSIBLE SCHOOL OF SUPREME VILLAINY! MUAHAHAHAHA!!!** (Be sure to include "MUAHAHAHAHA" and the exclamation points.)

- The gymnasium will be converted into my throne room and two students will fan me with fresh palm fronds at all times.

- From now on, when a student scores 100% on a test, they will be said to have **"VORDAKED"** it.

- Lipwartz and Waxclog will be fired.

- Career Day will be reinstated and I will be in charge of scheduling the parent speakers.

— VORDAK THE INCOMPREHENSIBLE

Okay, so apparently I didn't have quite the level of power I thought I did. Which is to say I didn't have any power at all. As it turns out, being the class president is actually a big pain in the hindquarters. I had to run the student council meetings, which typically centered around important issues such as whether to serve oatmeal or chocolate chip cookies at the orchestra recital. And if I got into an argument with another member of the student council, I didn't even have the option of activating a trapdoor beneath their chair and dropping them into a vat of molten titanium. Honestly, I don't see how they get anything done around here.

That colossal creep Combover rejected all but one of my demands. I could not erect a statue of myself anywhere in the school. Or a bust on a pedestal. Or even a plaque, certificate, or ribbon. I was told the only place I could display personal items was inside my locker, but, as you can see on the next page, it was already full.

On the bright side, he did think Career Day was a good idea. I received the go-ahead to schedule any parents with non-boa-constrictor-related jobs to come in and speak to the school every fourth Tuesday . . . beginning the following week! Now it was just a matter of inviting the good Commander.

I knew getting Virtue to flaunt himself before an auditorium full of adoring students wouldn't be difficult, but I was surprised when his acceptance letter showed up at the school that same day, before he had even been invited. He must have delivered it himself. I have no idea how he even knew we were having an assembly. He must have Career Day–sensing equipment of some

sort in that highfalutin headquarters of his. I wish I had known about this years ago—I could have saved the time I spent painstakingly plotting his capture and just hung a CAREER DAY sign over the door to my crocodile pit.

Dear Faculty and Students of Frederick Farding Junior High School,

I would be happy to attend your forthcoming Career Day. As you know, I am exactly what every young person should aspire to be. Will they make it? Of course not. They don't have my granite jaw. Or my amazing hair. Or any superpowers. But they can certainly spend the rest of their lives trying to reach my impossibly glorious standard—that's what's important.

Yours in the name of Justice,

P.S. — I will have autographed pictures available afterward for $10 each.

Can you believe this guy? Have you ever heard someone so full of himself? I mean . . . "glorious"?

Of course it was! What does that have to do with what I'm talking about here? *Focus!* The important thing is he would be here on Tuesday and, despite his inflated opinion of himself, it would be the last Career Day that leotard-wearing lamebrain would ever experience! MUAHAHAHAHA!!!

. . . .

Back at the lair, it was yet *another* unsuccessful day of freeze-ray testing! I had given that unproductive pigeonhead of a professor far more chances than he deserved. I usually only give one. Sometimes, less than that. In fact, I've been known to assign a task to a henchman or minion and then lower him into a vat of boiling cream cheese before he even has the *chance* to complete it. It keeps the rest of them on their toes.

This time, I didn't bother to enter the laboratory. The sound of Cranium sobbing on the other side of the door told me all I needed to know about his continuing failure. I just slipped the note under the door.

Hey, you blundering blockhead. How about firing your "Freeze Ray" into this tub of ice water so I can take a nice, hot bath? Ha!

– Vordak

P.S. – Meet me at the piranha tank in 20 minutes! MUAHAHAHAHA!!!

My patience had run out for the unproductive professor and his freeze-ray fiascos, so I hooked him up to my diabolically clever yet extremely slow-acting death trap—Piranha Tank Version. I handed him the freeze ray, pulled the start lever, and left the room. As he was slowly lowered headfirst into that tank of ill-tempered fish, one of two things would happen. If he could get the ray to work in time, he would be able to save himself. If so, I would have a Fantastically Frigid Freeze Ray that actually froze things, and my EVIL PLAN for taking over the world would be back on course. If he couldn't get it to function properly, I would have one less incompetent Evil Scientist to worry about. Sure, I would have to hold off on my planetary-takeover plan for a few weeks, but it would be worth the delay to rid myself of that sorry excuse for a supergenius. Either way was fine with me at this point.

When I say *slow-acting* death trap, I mean it. I passed the time by sending out invitations to the other parents who were chosen to attend Career Day. I also played a few hundred more rounds of Superhero Shin Kick. And then it was time to check in on Professor Cranium.

ZOUNDS! He had done it!

well done, Cranium – although I would probably have chosen to freeze the water in the tank instead.

– Vordak

p.s. – meet me at the crocodile pit when you thaw out

p.s.s. – just kidding, you gullible goober.
        meet me in your laboratory. And bring the ray.

CHAPTER NINE

Yesterday

I used my Villainous Voice Synthesizer to disguise my voice and call in sick yesterday. I originally grabbed my Villainously Vulgar Voice Synthesizer by mistake, but, luckily, Miss Fnarbarbler screamed and slammed the phone down before I had a chance to say who was calling.

With Commander Virtue's Career Day Comeuppance all set for the next day, I required time to prepare my Dreaded Dadbot. I had a number of robot types from which to choose and decided to go with my HAND-2000V **H**ighly **A**dvanced **N**oseless **D**estructobot.

Of course, my Dadbot couldn't show up at school looking like that. It would need a disguise that would allow it to blend in with the other parents without raising suspicion. Fortunately, my dad had left a box of his old clothes sitting on a shelf in the basement.

I also needed the Fantastical Freeze Ray ready by tomorrow. Now that Cranium had finally gotten it to work, it was simply a matter of making it powerful enough to freeze Lake Chargoggagoggmanchaug-gagoggchaubunagungamaugg. He seemed much more at ease since his piranha-tank breakthrough and was moving forward with the confidence and determination of a true Evil Genius. Just so he knew all his good work wasn't going unnoticed, I made sure to call him a worthless wormbrain, a dimwitted dunce, and a chimp-faced chowderhead several times before I left his laboratory.

CHAPTER TEN

Today

Which brings us up to date, back in the auditorium. Perhaps now that you know what I went through to get to this point, you can truly appreciate what you are about to witness.

"I'm sorry. Could you repeat that last part?"

I said "you can truly appreciate—"

"No, I mean starting with where you pulled the tuna over that kid's head."

WHAT?! That was seventy-nine pages ago! *You haven't been paying attention?!* Why, you little . . .

"Hey! Relax! I was kidding. Commander Virtue is right— you can't take a joke."

You *know* Commander Virtue?!

"Nah. I saw it on his blog."

Oh. So, anyway, here I sit, ready to witness the most terrifyingly tumultuous Tuesday the world has ever known! Cranium worked through the night and was able to complete the freeze ray, so I have decided to make this the *MOST MISERABLY MOMENTOUS DAY IN THE MEMORY OF MANKIND*! In the course of the next few hours I shall:

1. Defeat Commander Virtue!

2. Retrieve the balsoid coil and return to a younger, stronger, more vibrant *adult* version of myself!

3. Turn my Fantastically Frigid Freeze Ray upon humanity and take command of the planet!

4. Watch my *Toy Story 3* DVD (time permitting)!

In honor of this delightfully diabolical day, I have decided to record the forthcoming evil events live, as they happen. No other method would do my maniacal magnificence justice. At this very moment I am seated in the front row, notebook in hand, awaiting the Career Day speech of Commander Virtue himself.

My original plan was to sit way in back, behind Lars Widebritches, so Virtue wouldn't see me and be tipped off that something was up. But earlier in the day, he unexpectedly passed right by me in the hallway and didn't even seem to notice me. Yes, it's been a few years, and sure, my current stature is a bit unremarkable, but still, I *am* Vordak the Incomprehensible. I must admit, his snub hurt. However, since he didn't recognize me, I decided to sit right up front so that, when my Dadbot finishes with him, I can taunt him in a supremely Supervillainous manner and let him know exactly who was responsible for his ultimate demise! MUAHAHAHAHA!!!

Besides, Benny Yoshida was sitting behind Widebritches. My little show-and-tell friend had become queasy after scarfing Yoshida down in science class that day and threw him up on the way home from school. And this is the same little show-and-tell friend that counts sewer water and pond scum among his favorite treats.

Ingmar's dad spoke already, and he sounded like your typical fireman—"Don't play with matches. Check the batteries in your smoke detector. Don't deep-fry an eel over forty-eight inches long on the kitchen stove. Yada, yada, yada." Zounds, for a guy who carries an ax around with him all day, he sure seems to have something against the destruction of property.

Things are moving right along. Tuvier just introduced my Dreaded Dadbot. I need this to go off without a hitch, so I programmed his speech myself.

So far, so good!

Hey, I tried to write a speech about accounting, but it was just too boring. So I threw in a few things about myself to spice things up a bit. The students seem very impressed. Anyway, he's wrapping up now, so Virtue will be on soon.

Well, that went rather well, if I do say so myself. And I do. So it did. Best of all, no one suspects a thing, least of all the cretinous Commander. He looked directly at me numerous times during my Dadbot's speech and still nothing. Not so much as a flinch or a furrowed brow. *And now he is approaching the podium! A life free of Commander Virtue is within my grasp at last!* **I am so excited I feel as though I might burst!** I really should have used the restroom before I sat down.

My Dreaded Dadbot is programmed to attack Virtue the first time he utters the word *JUSTICE*. And he typically utters it two or three times per sentence, so this shouldn't take very long. Yes! It appears that square-jawed scumball is ready to begin!

AT LONG LAST I HAVE DONE IT! Virtue is a pathetic, quivering mass, and the boos and cupcakes should come raining down upon him at any moment! I . . . *wait a minute.* Why is he smoking like that? And what is that purple liquid leaking out of his nostrils? No! This cannot be! That isn't Virtue at all—it's *a robot*!

Well, that explains why he didn't recognize me. What a rotten thing to do—sending a robot to school disguised as a human. And now there appears to be something happening at the far end of the stage. Mrs. Tuvier is . . . *unscrewing her own head*?! That's not part of my plan—nor is it something I would recommend. She's going to . . .

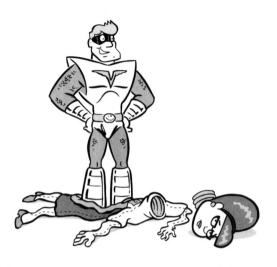

GREAT GASSY GOBLINS! Mrs. Tuvier is actually Commander Virtue! No wonder she graded so hard! And, now that I think about it, *Tuvier* is simply *Virtue* spelled sideways! I should have seen this coming a mile away.

As I had planned, the stage is being bombarded with boos and cupcake projectiles. This is unfortunate for a couple of reasons:

1. They are being directed at my Dadbot.

2. When I baked the cupcakes, I used cement powder instead of flour—what can I say? I thought they were going to be hurled at Commander Virtue.

But all is not lost. Things can still go according to my EVIL PLAN. I just need the real Virtue to say the word *justice*.

Justness? Did he say "just*ness*"? After decades of having to listen to that self-centered superstiff drone on about "*JUSTICE* this" and "*JUSTICE* that," did I really just hear him say "*JUSTNESS*"?! *Now Virtue is moving across the stage toward my Dreaded Dadbot, and it's just standing there, motionless! He's lifting it over his head and twirling it around and now it looks like he's going to . . . Oooh, that's not good. . . .*

Ack! What self-respecting Superhero changes his most beloved heroic utterance this late in his career? For the love of Fragnor, will his luck never run out? I had best beat a hasty retreat back to my lair amid all the confusion. It's only a matter of time before . . . *Wait another minute!* Now Principal Combover is unscrewing *his* head! I never figured Combover as being the sharpest knife in the drawer, but this still seems a bit . . .

It's Professor Cranium! And he has the Fantastically Frigid Freeze Ray! The day will yet be mine! Not even Commander Virtue can withstand my remarkable ray's icy onslaught. He's closing in on Virtue. Good thinking, Cranium. You don't want to risk missing your target. Okay, Cranium, that's close enough! Cranium, you're getting *too* close. Cranium, any closer and you might as well just hand him the darn freeze ray!

Cranium, *you just handed him the darn freeze ray*!

That backstabbing brainiac has now moved over to the podium and he's saying something to the students. He says he is tired of being treated poorly by evildoers like Vordak the Incomprehensible and has decided he wants to use his brain's frontal, temporal, AND occipital lobes for good.

And to think, just last week I got him a new iPad.

Now I have no choice but to flee.

Uh-oh! Commander Virtue has spotted me! He's rushing over! He has me in his infernal grasp and is hauling me back up onto the stage. And now he is about to remove my helmet! You are probably wondering how I am still able to write.

Ha! I told Myron H. I would give him a brand-new industrial-strength label maker if he wore my spare costume to the assembly. That's me, disguised as Myron H., making my way to the exit. In all the confusion, no one noticed me leave.

If my writing seems a bit hurried at this point it's because I am in the process of running back home to my lair. My foolproof EVIL PLAN to rid the world of Commander Virtue has failed, even though I specifically included the word *foolproof* in the plan's name. My EVIL PLAN to conquer the planet using my Fantastically Frigid Freeze Ray has also failed, which is a bit more understandable since I never declared that one to be foolproof. But at least I still have good old Evil Plan 1794, where I retrieve the balsoid coil from the school kitchen using my science-fair matter transporter. After what just happened, I obviously can't show my face in school again, so I may as well grab the coil, repair my Abominable Age-Reduction Ray, and return to adulthood to plot my revenge—right after *SpongeBob*. All right—time to stop writing so I can concentrate on running.

· · · · · · · · · · ·

Okay, I'm back safe and sound deep within the bowels of my underground lair. It's time to retrieve the balsoid coil, and I have decided to use the video capabilities of my Vordak Orb, or VORB, to record the event. That way, future generations of Supervillains will have the opportunity to witness my one-of-a-kind wonderfulness in action.

"Hey, wait a minute. Isn't that the same VORB that was in your Dadbot?"

I have two. I'm sending this one through the matter transporter as we speak. When it arrives in the school kitchen, it will position itself to properly capture my arrival on video.

Obviously, that means the VORB isn't here at the lair to record my departure. That task now falls to Little Vince Sminion and his cell-phone camera. Did I mention that the Sminion brothers work for me full-time now? As it turns out, they are both over eighteen and thus perfectly legal henchman material. I'll have Little Vince take a few pictures as I enter the transporter pod so there is an accurate record of my departure for any Hollywood types who I allow to create a film of my life.

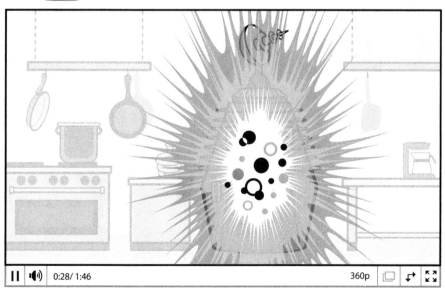

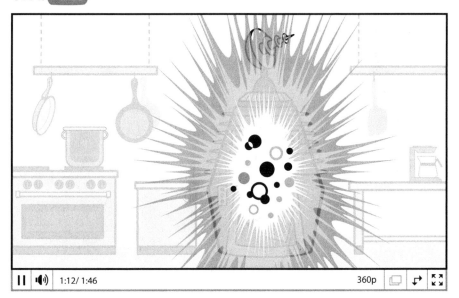

Vorb Tube

|| ◀))) 1:45/ 1:46   360p ⌷ ↷ ⤢

At last! The elusive balsoid coil is mine! MUAHAHAHAHA!!! Now to hand it over to Professor Cranium to install on my Abominable Age-Reduction Ray while I take a nap. I'm exhausted.

"Umm, Professor Cranium is off opposing evil somewhere with Commander Virtue."

Zounds, that's right! I *told* you I was exhausted. I'll just have to do it myself, then. I'll be right back. Keep yourself busy by repeating the phrase "Vordak Rules, Virtue Drools!" over and over until I return.

▪ ▪ ▪ ▪ ▪ ▪ ▪ ▪ ▪ ▪

Unfortunately, the last incident with the ray destroyed the power cord, so I had to run to the hardware store and get four thousand "AA" batteries, which were not included. I also sent the Sminion brothers to the city dump to dispose of the matter-transporter pod from the lair. The refrigerator disguise worked so well that somebody had put a tray of uncooked fish fillets in the kitchen pod and they transported back to the lair with me—I'd never have been able to get the stink out.

But now everything is set—the balsoid coil is in place and the age-alteration knob has been set to +15 YEARS. I have double- and triple-checked every meter, and I've taken every possible detail into account before stepping onto the platform of my age-altering ray. So now, gaze in wonder as I, Vordak the Incomprehensible, transform myself into a lean, mean, world-conquering machine!

Okay, I may have forgotten *one* tiny detail. Great Gassy Goblins! When they say "tightie whities," they aren't kidding! Repeat that *Rules / Drools* thing a few more times while I go ahead and change into my other outfit.

■ ■ ■ ■ ■ ■ ■ ■ ■ ■ ■

That's better! I can actually feel the strength and energy coursing through my mature yet youthful body!

"To be honest, you don't look any different than you did at the beginning of the book."

Well, of course I do! Just look at the puff of my chest! And the fit of my tights! Now, could I go for a few more sit-ups to firm up the mid-section just a bit?

Sure, but there is no denying that my appearance is even more splendificent than it was before I began this adventure.

I am awe-inspiring! I am powerful! I am back and I'm bad and I'm ready to conquer humanity and RULE THE WORLD! And this time NO ONE WILL STOP ME!

"What about Commander Virtue?"

OKAY—NO ONE ELSE WILL STOP ME!

AHAHAHAHAH**AHAH**

HAHAHAHAHAHA

HAHAHAHA ... oops

About the Author

VORDAK THE INCOMPREHENSIBLE is a world-class Supervillain and the Evil Master of all he surveys. His first book, *Vordak the Incomprehensible: How to Grow Up and Rule the World* has inspired a whole new generation of minions and fiends. His current whereabouts are unknown (and no, they are not in his parents' basement in Trenton, New Jersey). You are hereby instructed to visit Vordak online at www.vordak.com, and he will know if you don't, so beware.

About the Minions

SCOTT SEEGERT was selected to transcribe Vordak's notes based on his ability to be easily captured. He has completely forgotten what fresh air smells like and has learned to subsist on a diet of beetles, shackle rust, and scabs. As far as he knows, he still has a wife and three children in southeast Michigan.

JOHN MARTIN had the great misfortune of being chosen by Vordak to illustrate this book. He hasn't seen the sun in three years and spends his free time counting down the months to his annual change of underwear. The last he heard, he also had a wife and three children living in southeast Michigan.

IF YOU ENJOYED THIS VICIOUSLY VILLAINOUS VOLUME, YOU MAY BASK FURTHER IN MY BRILLIANCE (AND LEARN A THING OR TWO ABOUT EVIL!) WITH

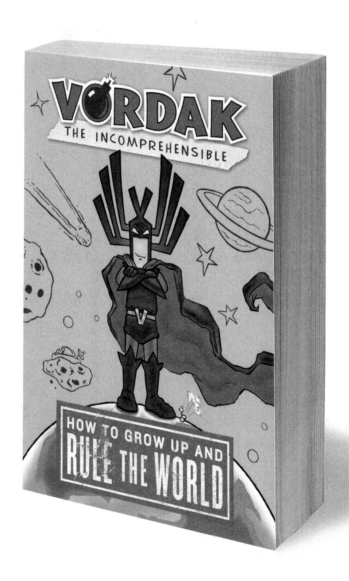